WORTH THE RISK

LAKE SPARK SERIES
BOOK 1

EVEY LYON

LAKE SPARK SERIES

Worth the Risk

Worth the Chance

Worth the Wait

ABOUT

Coach Hudson Arrows wants to sweep Piper off her feet. The fact she's his niece's best friend? May just send him into overtime.

A scorching one-night stand with a stranger was supposed to be my night of adventure to enjoy and move on. I didn't expect that a few weeks later my friend would introduce said stranger as the man walking her down the aisle because he's her godfather and uncle. And I certainly didn't expect him to be a famous football coach who insists I escape with him to his small-town lake house for a rendezvous. He may be old enough to be my dad, but the man's charisma is a winning touchdown straight to my lust-filled heart.

We keep our relationship a secret.

It doesn't take long for me to realize that there is more to Hudson than his dirty-talking mouth and his persistence that I may be what he's been waiting for. What we have turns into something I didn't bargain for. But I'm not blind to what's at stake once the world finds out about us. And I'm not sure if it's Hudson or me trying to convince us more, that together, we may just be worth the risk...

Hudson and Piper bring the heat into this age-gap, slightly forbidden, and completely swoonworthy story. Worth the Risk is book one in the standalone interconnected Lake Spark series. For lovers of small-town romance with a touch of sports.

HUDSON

The glass of whiskey, neat, slides my way against the bar, and I'm quick to accept the amber-colored liquid. I examine the contents for a second or two, but I don't need to debate it long. I know anything I drink here in this chic, industrial-styled restaurant and bar will be good, and I've had a long day.

After hours of meetings with team management, my brain feels like it may be fried.

"Anything else, Hudson? I'm going to close up early." Wes is the owner of Jupiter, the bar I frequent because the hospitality is excellent, the food is star-worthy, and this place is crawling with Chicago's sports elite even on a slow day—well, except tonight. Right now, it's just me.

I shake my head. "It's all good. I'll drink up then head out."

"No rush. I need to do some paperwork upstairs anyway, plus the weather is that horrible cold rain, so I'm trying to avoid it." Wes is in his early thirties and has a personality that welcomes conversation.

"Why are you even behind the bar?" I wonder aloud, as

he is normally up in his office and only circles the restaurant a few times when high-profile guests are here.

He grins. "Because I'm a good boss and sent my staff home early since it wasn't busy. Plus, when I saw you come in, then I figured I might try to get some intel for a few football bets that I have going on with friends."

His humor causes me to tip my head up, with a smirk forming. "I won't be divulging any secrets, but The Winds will have a good year."

Our draft was just announced, and it's May, which means we still have training season ahead before deciding our final roster, and I'm prepared to work those boys into the ground, as I have a record to uphold.

"You are the team's coach, so you may be biased," he counters.

I sigh at the reminder. I love my job, but damn, the pressure some days is a lot. Being a star quarterback back in my heyday was tough, but being a coach in a city driven by sports? Fucking insanity. I question my decision to take this job daily, especially if we lose a game and half the city is cursing my name, but then I get to the field or watch a player excel and I'm hooked all over again.

The sound of the revolving door swooshing open catches our attention. The umbrella, with a pattern that looks like dancing lobsters on it, is obstructing our view of the person beneath, but the sound of heels pattering is enough to tell me that it's a woman.

"Sorry, we're closed," Wes calls out just as the umbrella collapses.

Now I have a full view, and I'm not sure where to start.

The woman has deep-pink heels, and her skirt falls just below her knee, but damn, it is tight. Working my way up her body, I intend to give her the full once-over. Her black jacket is open, and I get a glimpse of a blouse that matches her shoes. Then her lips have a similar color, and they part open, and I just want to do a double take because she is easy on the eyes.

"Oh." She nearly frowns. "That's a shame. I was hoping for an escape from this weather. It's been quite a day."

Wes seems to study her for a second, possibly because my eyes haven't drifted off her for more than a millisecond.

"You know what… one drink," he offers.

A smile stretches on her lips, and she walks in our direction with a sway that seems to be restricted, probably by the fact that her skirt is the type of fabric that must rip easily, and no, I'm not proud that my brain made that connection. She slides her jacket off and places it on the back of the stool, then sits next to me as she swipes a strand of her long, light brown hair behind her ear.

"Let me guess, gin and tonic?" I ask her to make conversation.

She shyly smiles at me. "No. I'm a martini, classic, with three olives kind of gal."

"Coming right up." Wes begins to gather the ingredients.

She holds her hand up to stop. "Wait, can I just have a Shirley Temple?" She nearly groans as she says it.

I scoff a sound. "I wouldn't have expected that choice." I set my glass to the side and then angle my stool in her direction.

"Believe me, I wish it was the martini, but I just remembered that I promised a friend to join her on the no-alcohol-for-a-week train. She wants her mind clear for when her boyfriend proposes, because she feels like it's going to happen any day now," she explains.

"Wow, friendship. But you look like you could use the martini," I highlight the obvious.

Her head lolls to the side ever so slightly. "True." She taps her fingers on the counter. "Ugh, I guess my day trumps maybe-proposals. Martini, please." Wes nods then gets busy with making her drink. Her eyes brighten, and God, I love the curve of her cheeks. "Martinis are my grandmother's favorite. Every day at three after her soaps, for as long as I can remember, it's been her routine. It's traditional, I like that."

"You don't seem like a traditional girl."

The sound of the martini shaker stops just as this woman's brow raises. I realize my tone may have been... playful. But it doesn't matter, because for a moment, we look at one another, our blue eyes connecting, and recognize that we're both taken off guard by this unusual vibration in the air.

Admittedly, it normally takes a lot for someone to make me pause. I'm not easily affected—well, except tonight, it seems.

A smirk plays on her lips, and it feels like it's her slow ease into my presence. "Something like that." She examines me for a second then rests her chin in her hand, her elbow propped on the counter. "What brings you here on a Tuesday evening?"

"Long workday."

"So I gathered. You're wearing a suit yet no tie, which means you took it off at the end of the day. What do you do?"

Wes places a martini on a napkin in front of this woman. "Not a sports fan?" He seems surprised that she doesn't seem to know who I am.

She thanks him with a nod before she entwines her fingers, with perfectly polished pink nails, around the stem of the glass. "No. I know zero about any sport. Why?"

I fucking love that answer. Mostly because during my history as a star player turned one of the youngest coaches with the highest paycheck, I got a title in the press as bona fide bachelor. There have been a lot of women who wanted to hang off my arm for the cameras too.

But to this woman, I'm an unknown.

Nor could she probably figure it out just by looking at me. I'm tall but not overly so, and I'm not bulky, as my career was based on speed and escaping tackles. I keep myself fit, unlike many former players turned coach.

Clearing my throat, I offer my hand. "I'm Hudson, by the way. And let's just say I work with numbers and physics." Partially true. Today's management meeting was all numbers, and we make plays based on aerodynamics.

After a sip from her drink, she frees her hand from her glass and offers me a few fingers to shake. "Piper. I know, it's such a ridiculous name."

Letting her soft, delicate digits go, I give her a confused look. "Why? I like it. It's cute."

Piper rolls her eyes. "Exactly. Cute. I don't know, I feel like people associate it with, like, a little gingerbread person or something."

I laugh at her thought. "Okay, I could see that connection but only because you point it out." Leaning against the back of my stool, I grab my drink once more and get comfortable for a conversation that I feel like I'm going to have with Piper.

"Anyways, thanks for letting me crash your moment of solitude. It was a day from hell."

"How so?" Another sip of whiskey hits my mouth.

Her head bobs slightly to the side, as if she's debating how much information to share, then she seems to shake off the thought. "I was battling it out with a shipping company for something I ordered, fabric that I've been waiting on, and they said someone would drop it off between nine and five, but no one did. I decided to take it into my own hands and marched right down to their office in hopes of getting my package. Nothing. Then Chicago spring decided to laugh at me and pour down freezing rain. It isn't even a full moon, and my aura is really fucked up right now."

She's slightly quirky, and I like that.

"You were running in heels around town in this weather?" I'm impressed.

Her mouth is closed, but it just makes her wry smile sexier. "You never know when you need to be rescued and hopefully by a hot fireman." She winks at me.

I tip my glass in her direction. "Points for surviving in this weather."

"I'm going to head upstairs to look at some paperwork," Wes says in my direction. "Just let yourself out when you're done?"

"Sure."

"Oh, I owe you for the martini." Piper moves to grab her bag.

I touch her arm to stop her from digging into her purse. "Nah, it's fine. It's on me, and Wes will add it to my tab."

Piper flashes me an appreciative look.

Wes clears his throat and gives me an awkward yet entertained smile. He seems to know that either Piper or I are in trouble, the kind that I haven't had in a while. Life has been a little crazy for me, to say the least.

I give a nod to Wes before returning my fully invested attention to Piper. "Fabric. You work with clothing?"

She nods and plays with her last olive on a skewer, and Christ, she sucks that fruit with perfection. "Yes, I'm a designer, actually."

"Yeah? Dresses?" My lips land on the rim of my glass, then the moment liquid hits my throat, I nearly choke because

I swear I just heard her say *lingerie*. Swallowing with great effort, my eyes don't blink. "Did you just say lingerie?"

"Yep," Piper proudly replies. "Well, more pajamas, with a special soft cotton fabric and lace trim, but now I'm venturing into evening attire. That is, well… I'll leave it to your imagination."

Fuck me, I only heard lace, and she said it with such simple confidence.

"So, you mentioned numbers, what exactly do you do?" she asks.

"You know, let us stay vague on details. We've both had a tough day, and I'm enjoying our conversation too much to bring work into the mix," I suggest.

She chuckles and throws her olive skewer to the side. "Enjoying our conversation?" She contemplates my answer and taps her fingers on the napkin. "Do you think I'm flirting with you?"

Now I have to laugh. "No. Should I be offended? I mean, am I not flirtable?"

Her cheeks raise and turn a shade of pink. "It's not that. I just don't want you to think I walk into bars and try to pick up random older men. Not that you're old or ancient, I mean, you must be, what, ten years older than me? I'm rambling. That happens sometimes. Sorry." She seems flustered.

I love this woman's honesty and ability to speak her mind. It's refreshing and much like myself. I kind of thrive from speaking openly and making others feel uncomfortable to push their limits toward what I know they are capable of. Except in this moment, while Piper thinks I must be offended, I'm the opposite.

I instantly reach out and touch her elbow. "Relax. Breathe." She responds to my request and seems to calm. "I don't think you're a high-class hooker if that's what you were implying, and I'm happy to hear that I'm not ancient."

Her face turns red in embarrassment. "You're in good shape. How old are you, can I ask?"

"Forty-two. You?"

"Twenty-five and ordering children's cocktails, really demonstrating my maturity here."

"It's okay, you got to the martini in the end, and I won't highlight that I'm old enough to be your dad," I inform her. Consciously, I leave out the fact that I do have a son her age, but for now, I don't want the age factor to be a deterrent for her to walk away sooner than later tonight.

"As long as you don't ask me to call you daddy." She says it so casually as she takes a sip of her drink, but the moment she realizes what she said, her face turns cherry red. "Oh my God, I did not just say that. I need to stop jabbering." She seems mortified.

Her sense of humor makes me grin. I like that her mind may be unintentionally dirty.

Leaning in closer to her, I tease her. "It's okay, I prefer *sir* anyhow." I run my tongue along the inside of my mouth because I'm trying to restrain my enjoyment in this unexpected evening.

She looks at me, impressed with my counter remark, and her smirk grows comfortable again before she nibbles her bottom lip.

Something inside of me is eager to push her buttons. "Do I make you nervous, Piper?" I hear the hint of determination in my voice. A need to explore the curiosity that this woman sparks inside me.

I notice her throat bob with a swallow, but then she sits up straight with confidence. "No, Hudson, you don't." Her tone is sinfully delicious and firm. I bet she could be a little vixen because her tone was pure challenge.

She doesn't blink, and I'm drawn into the deep blue of her eyes that has me thanking the fact that this place is lit just right so I can figure out the exact color of her eyes as they seem now more green.

"Do your eyes magically change color with the light?" I ask her, as we seem to be locked in a stare.

"Not that I know of." Her eyes sideline to her martini, and she is quick to pick it up.

"I take it there's no man to tell you on a daily basis if your eyes are casting a spell on him."

She tries to suppress a smile. "That is a ridiculous line, and you know it."

I chuckle under my breath. "You're right. But for some reason tonight, cheesy lines are rolling off my tongue."

Actually, a sort of light ignites inside of me. I've been so focused on everyone else that I forgot that I'm allowed to have a connection with someone on a physical level. Piper is the perfect reminder, and I think that I'm enamored with her.

"If that cheesy line was your subtle way of asking if I have a boyfriend, you are a little late in the conversation to be requesting that information." The remainder of her drink disappears as she knocks back the glass then slides it back onto the bar.

"Why is that?"

"I doubt you would smirk the way you do if you thought I was off the market."

We study one another, and I feel my pulse quicken. Call me a savage, but I think I want to throw her onto the countertop and lick her like she did her olives. This woman has the ability to steal my breath and make me laugh, and for that reason, I want to make her scream.

But instead, we chat for the next fifteen minutes about the city and food. My cheeks may hurt from laughing at every retort we bounce off one another in conversation.

I look at my watch. I know we need to get out of here soon. Piper seems to notice too that our night may be wrapping up—well, not if I have anything to say about it.

"You're intriguing, but I don't know why. I only just met you," she says.

The corner of my mouth curves up. "Ah, so you are attracted to me."

Piper doesn't answer but looks away with a sheepish grin. "Do you do this with all the women you meet?"

"I'm not doing anything, darling, except talking to a beautiful woman who seems to be enjoying my company… and no, I don't make it a habit of taking a woman to the hotel across the street." Geez, even I recognize the swagger in my voice.

Her eyes widen from my statement. "Wow, how did a hotel come into this conversation?"

"We wouldn't last the extra twenty minutes it would take to get to my place. Plus, it's fucking raining." I look at her with a piercing gaze because I can't look away from this creature who sauntered into my life on a mundane Tuesday.

"Why am I not walking away from this?" she asks herself with a fixed smile because we are being two ridiculous souls acting in a way that I know neither one of us is accustomed to. Because despite the many offers I get, I don't pick up women in bars. I mean, I'm not completely a saint, but I would say I have a 75% moral conscience when it comes to pursuing women. Yet right now, I'm feeling on edge because I want her, and I'm pulling out my cocky card which could be a risky move.

"Why am I acting like a man already addicted?" I softly

ponder the truth. She is like something I've never had a taste of, and I recognize a warning in my head that Piper may just pull me in a direction that I'm not used to.

I glance down as I begin to draw circles with my fingertip on her hand that's resting on the bar. Her skin is silky, and I feel her body tense, but not in a bad way. She's surprised maybe by the magnetic attraction that we seem to have.

My eyes draw a line up to her face when she blows out a deep breath. "You have some smooth lines, Hudson. I'm really wondering why the red flag isn't flashing in my head yet." She looks down at my fingers, intrigued. "I'm normally a 'trip to the candy store when I'm stressed' kind of person. I've never tried sleeping with a stranger to let out some bad-day vibes."

"Do you believe in trying everything once?"

"I do… yes."

I move farther into her space and closer to her ear, now letting my hand travel up her arm to touch her hair. "Listen, we need to get out of here. I'm not a serial killer, Wes has seen you with me, you can text a friend, and we can go across the street. Drink, talk, I don't care, but you're curious about something and so am I."

She glances to me, her head angling in a way that brings her mouth near my own. Mint, she smells of peppermint. Her warm breath hits my skin. "Tempting."

Our lips dance on their own accord. She's drawing me in, and I really am questioning why I feel like a man who would get on his knees to beg for this woman. Something in the air feels unique, and it started the moment she walked through the door.

"Do you always make men crazy?" I whisper.

"Do you always make women do things they wouldn't normally do?"

I scoff. "Make? No. Wanting something out of their comfort zone? Completely."

She points a finger at me. "I'm taking a chance that you aren't a murderer." A grin spreads on her mouth before she hops off her chair and offers me her hand.

It was a quick check-in, no questions asked because they know me, as I stay here sometimes during the season instead of my place in the city. In no time, we find ourselves walking down the hall to the room.

I spin her until her back hits the wall near the door. I cradle her face between my hands and hold her firmly in place so her mouth is on offer.

This isn't what I was expecting today. And by the fact that Piper is breathing heavy, then I would say this is a surprise for her too.

My eyes are fixed on her gorgeous mouth, the one I'm about to devour.

"Do we need a safe word or something?" She tries to contain her laugh. Her ability to keep the mood light is a trait that I adore.

"Fuck me," I murmur. "I really want to know where your imagination just went."

She wraps her hands around my waist under my open suit jacket. "I'm not sure. You're kind of consuming my thoughts, and then I realize you're standing right in front of me."

"And I'm going to kiss you."

I lean down and capture her mouth, an instant hit of lust and martini creating the only taste I want on my lips. My tongue swipes along the seam of her mouth, and she willingly opens her lips to offer me more. Our spark creates a wildfire that will burn down the entire earth... okay, crazy talk hitting me.

I pull her tight to my body, our lips never parting, then lift her slightly up as I stretch my arm out with the keycard. We find our way inside the luxurious suite, and the moment we finally create space between us, Piper takes in her surroundings, her lips swollen.

She notices the chilled champagne in a bucket. "Who are you? We literally checked in only five minutes ago and already this is here. Not to mention, I noticed security give you a nod." Her question is more amused than curious.

I walk to the bottle as she continues toward the floor-to-ceiling window overlooking the city. Damn, she is a scene. She takes no notice of me as she looks out and tosses her jacket to the side. Even when I pop the cork on the champagne, she doesn't flinch. Instead, she seems mesmerized by the view, at peace even.

"No champagne for me. I want to do this before I lose my nerve." She glances over her shoulder in my direction.

I pause my work on the bottle. "You know, we can just talk." I feel a need to reassure her, touch base, and to be honest, just sharing the same air in this room with her is enough to put me at ease and make my night.

We don't need to do more. But her in my arms, preferably naked, would be even better.

She turns around and begins to stroll slowly in my direction. "Talk?" She tilts her head with an adorable laugh. "After that kiss? Not a fucking chance." Then she springs into my arms.

My cock rises to the occasion, happy with her choice. Our lips are all over one another, and I debate fast or slow.

Slow.

Fast.

This is like an aggravating play in the scrimmage zone, but at least I know that I'm going to get the touchdown.

Her sounds are lost in our mixed breaths, and I have my answer.

"Slow," I say.

Setting her down, taking her wrists gently in my hands to hold them up, I look down at her thinking she is way too beautiful to be alone for a Tuesday night. Whoever let her go is a moron, but I should send him box seats because it means I get to have her now.

"Let me take something off," she whispers with a seductive grin.

I bring my finger to glide along her cheek. "You do that, then look out at the view that you were admiring."

"Yes, *sir*," she teases me, and I have to shake my head again. "Sit down," she demands.

I love her confident effort to add to our dynamic, and I move to sit on the chaise lounge in the corner. I get comfortable, untuck my shirt from my pants, and begin to unbutton my shirt, with my eyes glued on the show.

She swipes her hair to one side, lifts her blouse off, then shimmies off her skirt. Her mint-green lace lingerie set is a sight for sore eyes, with the bra cups full, the color of lace a perfect contrast to her pink shoes. I could come just looking at her right now.

"An original?" I wonder as I squint my eyes as if it will magically magnify the view.

Her fingers cascade down her skin from her neck to between her cleavage. "Uh-huh, private collection in fact," she rasps.

"Lucky me. Do you have any idea how sexy you are?" I ask.

"I do." Piper has confidence, that's for sure. She flashes

me a coy look before walking to the window. "So, about that safe word…" She trails off.

Shaking my head ruefully, I grin, but I also can't control the urge inside me to consume her until she melts into the mattress.

I pounce off the seat and grab ice from the bucket on my way to Piper. I throw away a few cubes until I have one trapped between my fingers. Noticing the way her body shivers, her nipples pebble, and every inch of her is screaming to be discovered, I don't delay.

"Hands against the window, Piper," I order.

The moment her hands hit the glass, the piece of ice between my fingers lands on the side of her stomach, causing her to flinch as the ice begins to melt against the heat of her body.

I smirk to myself, wondering if she will ever figure out my connection to football. "Your safe word can be 'foul.'"

In response, she moans as I slide the ice lower.

2

PIPER

3 WEEKS LATER

My grandmother hands me the television remote control to set on the coffee table. We just spent an hour watching her favorite soap and sipping our martinis in her living room.

"You know, I haven't watched this in years and yet the same actors are still on there," I remark as I hold my near-empty glass out to the side.

My grandmother plays with her pearl necklace. "It's strangely comforting that I age with some of those characters. Anyways, what else is this old bat going to do?"

I chuckle at her thought. "What don't you do? Symphony, tea with the ladies from your book club, giving the doorman an earful. And you're not old. You haven't hit eighty yet, you have a few more years, and besides, eighty is the new seventy. You're hardly a dinosaur," I assure her.

"Piper, I would prefer you tell me that I'm a frail old lady who needs to see her only granddaughter married one day soon." She gives me a stern eye that only makes me smile more.

"I came here to spend quality time with you, my favorite senior citizen, and this is what I get?" I pretend to be offended.

She drinks every last drop of her drink before placing the glass on the side table which probably cost half my rent.

I can't help but glance into my near-empty glass. The last time I had one of these was a few weeks ago on that night that will go down in my life's history book as unforgettable and one of a kind.

Wild, magnetic, and I felt free.

I've never just hooked up with someone. For the first time in a long time, I felt an opportunity where I felt comfortable and grabbed it before I lost the chance.

I have zero regrets… okay, maybe one. But I don't think too long about that.

"At least tell me that you're having fun. A woman with your looks who is as successful as you shouldn't be spending nights alone." My face must look astonished that she's prying into my sex life, but dear old grandmama has always been bold. "Oh please, you think your grandfather—God rest his soul—was my first? Besides, I've seen your designs, and you must get your inspiration from somewhere."

"This conversation is not happening," I lament.

"Oh, dear, don't even try to hide the facts. You look like a woman who has seen more action than a Vegas showgirl."

There must be a giddy look on my face. It's because of Hudson and the moments from that night that have raced in and out of my head for the last few weeks. He had a command on me that I desire, and experience that I crave. Most of all, he could make me smile with our weird brand of humor.

Now I tip the glass to my lips and make it as dry as the Arizona desert. "It doesn't matter. There is nobody to bring to Friday-night dinner. I'm too busy for a relationship anyway."

"Piper, you're never too busy to find a husband or wife, whatever you fancy. And I mean someone who is a *real* contender and worthy of you." Her pointed look is the reminder of why I am perhaps hesitant, but she won't let me dwell over her reference for long, and I too move past it.

I sigh and put down my glass. "I literally thought 'oh, I could surprise my grandmother on this cloudy day with some cake and watch some soaps with her since I've worked hard all morning.' I'm very much regretting my choice."

She folds her hands together and places them on her lap, straightening her posture with a smirk on her face. "You're right, dear. Tell me, how are your designs? Did you try the new supplier yet?"

I purse my lips, because as much as everything is going well business-wise, it's a lot of to-do lists. "I think it's going to work. I need to see how the fabric stretches over the wiring of the bra of the new bodysuits, but the short loungewear jumpsuits with lace are selling like hot cakes."

My grandmother looks at me fondly. "I always knew you would carry on the tradition."

Now that is praise I can appreciate. Going back generations, my family came to the US from Europe. My great-grandfather was a tailor, my grandmother a seamstress turned corporate dressmaker, and she made a lot of money too. My mother skipped the tradition altogether, and well, me? I'm making my own path. I don't even use my grandmother's name, even though it would have given me an extra boost. Instead, I'm stuck with my father's last name. I'm Piper Dapper—it has a melody and makes me crazy at the same time.

I admire my grandmother; I grew up watching her pick beautiful fabrics while someone with a notebook would follow her around taking instruction. It rubbed off on me, and somewhere in college, I started designing comfortable pajamas with cute prints and the epitome of loungewear, but then... I started a special line of lingerie. My parents nearly spit out their wine at that family dinner when I told everyone, while my grandmother just clapped her hands together in celebration.

"I might need your help. I promised April I would design her wedding dress. She wants simple but elegant."

April is my best friend whom I met two years ago. April works in accounting, hates it, and is way too bubbly to be sitting behind a desk. We met in a jewelry-making workshop, and both realized we had no talent for bracelets, so instead, skipped the class and went for coffee instead. Over cupcakes and lattes, our friendship was solidified.

"She's engaged?"

I nod. "Yes. It happened a few weeks ago." While I was being fucked senseless. "They've been dating for a year, he's a lawyer."

"That's wonderful. Send her my congratulations and ask her where I should send the money to ensure she throws you the bouquet at the wedding." She's teasing me again.

I stand up, knowing I need to get going if I have any chance of meeting April for smoothies later. Then again, I probably shouldn't have had a martini at this time of day either. But everything is about balance.

My grandmother follows me as I make my way through her penthouse, past statues and art, until we reach her front door.

"You know I still have contacts at the big department stores if you want an in," she casually mentions.

"My answer is still no. The future is online stores, and plus, I would be much happier with a boutique anyhow," I remind her as I throw my purse strap over my shoulder.

We hug goodbye, and I'm on my merry way after I promise to visit again next week.

When I'm in the elevator going down, I smile to myself. Partly because a flashback hits me of being wrapped in a tangled mess of arms and limbs.

Then my mind remembers the way Hudson took me from behind while I held onto the bed for dear life. And fuck me, that man has a mouth that would make a hooker blush.

It was a good night.

A great night.

Excellent.

All the more reason why I hate myself for leaving before he even woke.

———

I FIND myself watching my friend approach the table.

"Has something happened, Ginger?" Only April can get away with calling me Ginger, a nickname that she insists on. My friend slides onto the seat in front of me. She has two smoothies in to-go cups and offers me the peanut-butter-banana one.

Quickly I sip from the straw before I burst with a reply that's been running in my head for weeks. "What do you mean?" I pretend that life is completely normal.

April slams her hand on the table, the strength of her amusement causing her blonde hair to fall around her grinning face. "Lately, you've been... daydreaming."

I play with my straw and avoid looking at my best friend

until I realize I will never be able to keep this from her. Originally, I said nothing because I wanted her to bask in her engagement and not steal the spotlight from her during our coffee chats.

"I kind of did something out of character a few weeks ago. On one night in particular." I bite my inner lip and then glance up at her.

April just stares at me, and I wait to see if she connects the dots.

"With someone," I clarify.

The moment she figures it out, her mouth gapes open. "No way!" I nod slowly. "Like, with a complete stranger?" She's grinning, clearly invested in this conversation.

"Yes, total. It just kind of happened. It was a long day, and then I went for a drink, which I ended up needing for the liquid courage because that man was something. And let me tell you, he lives up to the cliché of an older man being demanding in the bedroom."

Her eyes widen. "Older?"

I bob my head from side to side. "Yeah. I mean, he looks younger than he is, but I guess he is old enough to be my father."

April nearly spits out her smoothie. "What in the world happened to you? I mean, this is like that thirst trap from the Sound of Music because we all know Christopher Plummer as the Captain is probably what's fueling your need to sleep with an older man."

My face squinches together. "Although a classic, I assure you that was not my motivation."

She waves off my notion. "What else do you know about this guy?"

I debate telling her everything, but I know she would play

detective in a heartbeat. "Not much. It's the way it should be when it's a one-night stand. Anyways, I doubt I'll be seeing him again."

"Why?"

I awkwardly look away. "Because... I left before he woke up."

She slaps her hand onto her mouth in shock. "Who are you?"

Blowing out a breath, I wonder too. "I don't really know why I did it. I guess I was scared to face him in the morning. It was a great night and maybe I didn't want to deal with the disappointment that it was only that. We both went into the evening knowing it was a one-time thing, and I'm not accustomed to that protocol, so I guess I freaked out."

"So, it wasn't because of his skill set?" She flashes her eyes at me.

I can't hide my smile. "I mean..." I look around to make sure nobody is watching and lean into the table. "Against the window, on the bed in three different positions, and he went down on me twice. It was unreal."

April turns giddy. "You're still able to walk?"

"It happened a few weeks ago, and I didn't plan on ever telling you. Plus, you were in your engagement bliss," I explain.

"Does he have a name?"

My voice begins to form the syllables, but I'm interrupted by April's phone vibrating.

"Sorry, I need to take this. It's the restaurant for the party."

"It's okay. I need to head out anyway."

She answers her phone and touches my shoulder as she leaves the table because there is better reception out on the street. "I'll see you tomorrow at 7pm, sharp," she quickly whispers on the way out.

I salute her in response, relieved I didn't need to say Hudson's name, because then it would just remind me that the only thing I regret is not staying in the morning.

.

3

PIPER

Arriving at the restaurant on the seventeenth floor, I know why April would have picked this place for her engagement party. She is a complete foodie, and the chef at this new restaurant is all the rage.

I enter the private room where a large group is busy drinking, grabbing appetizers off of floating plates, and there's jazz playing in the background.

It doesn't take but a second before someone pulls my arm, and I turn to see April smiling brightly at me with her new blue dress. She looks ecstatic.

"There you are, Ginger!"

I adjust my small clutch purse in my hand that matches my pale peach wrap dress. "Sorry, took forever to get a taxi." I smile at her before we embrace for a hug. "You know I wouldn't miss this for the world."

We part and look at one another in an excited mood.

"Did you bring your mystery guy?" She flashes her eyes at me. "I didn't forget about that conversation."

I scoff. "You know I'm here alone because it was a one-time thing. We went over this."

"I still don't understand why you left. Maybe it would have been the most romantic breakfast of your life."

I touch her shoulders to refocus her attention. "Or maybe we should just talk about you marrying the man who gave you that rock on your finger."

She holds up her hand to admire the ring, and her smile grows wider still. "Jeff is around here somewhere. Half of his law firm I think are here. Anyways, I wanted to ask you something."

"Oh?"

She takes my hand and quickly guides me to a quiet spot away from the crowd, grabbing a present off a side table amongst all the gifts in the process. We keep moving until she stops us in a corner, with windows all around, which makes me feel like I'm half in the sky.

April hands me the small pink bag with a lot of ribbon. "I know you promised to design my dress."

I look up at her as I try to untie the bow. "I would much prefer you get a dress from a real wedding dress designer, and I can focus on what you wear on the honeymoon."

"Nothing. I'll wear nothing," she informs me one-toned.

"Fair point." I get the bow off and peek inside the tissue paper to see a small statue. A glass figurine of a lobster, dancing or in an odd pose. "What's this?" I'm puzzled.

"Thought my maid of honor would need something ridiculous for her design table, and I saw it at the market last weekend and thought of your umbrella."

"I'm maid of honor now?" I ask, half-surprised. She nods. "I guess if someone has to do it." I pretend like she's twisting my arm to help her out.

April shakes her head ruefully. "Funny. Okay, so I can check that off the list."

"You can. I accept my responsibility and will place this freaky statue somewhere," I confidently inform her.

"Great. We definitely should insist on weekly coffee meetings to go over all the wedding stuff and for me to hear if there is any chance of mystery guy making an appearance."

I roll my eyes. "Go. Go harass your other guests."

"I will." She grins. "I need to find my uncle anyway; I asked him to walk me down the aisle at the wedding."

"Oh yeah?" I was wondering who would do the job. April doesn't know who her father is because her mom did insemination with an anonymous donor.

"You've never met my Uncle Bay."

"Nope. You talked about him a few times."

April grabs my hand. "Well, then you should meet. It's only fitting since he's walking me down the aisle and you are walking ahead of me down the aisle. He's my godfather too."

"Sounds like he's the perfect man for the job then." I smile, happy for her.

She guides me through the crowd to a pair of men in dark jeans and blazers, with one visible to us and the other who has his back to us. They seem to be laughing about something, but when one man sees us approaching, he touches the other man's shoulder and leaves.

"Uncle Bay, I want you to meet my maid of honor," April announces as we circle around the man.

The moment my eyes draw a line up and land on the man in front of me, my entire body stills.

Those familiar strong hands are currently gripping a fine scotch. His jaw is cut sharp, yet experience makes me know that his nuzzling skills are excellent. I know there is a simple tattoo of an arrow on his shoulder underneath his shirt. Those blue eyes pierce me with surprise, plus something so tense… recognition. That mouth of his twitches barely, but I notice.

"Hudson?" I nearly squeak.

April immediately looks at me, confused.

"This is Ginger?" Hudson asks April, clearly also baffled by what's happening, yet I can't help but notice that he seems unnervingly calm, while internally my stomach just did a flip, and I may be pressing my thighs together in reaction to being in his presence, but whatever.

Looking between us, April smiles like we're crazy. "I mean, yes, this is Ginger. I call her that because her name is Piper, well, Piper Dapper, and she says her name reminds her of gingerbread people."

Now I see the corner of Hudson's mouth begin to hitch up because he knows that reference far too well.

April looks at me again, then touches her forehead like she forgot something. "I guess you recognize my uncle."

"Your Uncle Bay?" I look wide-eyed at April.

She nods her head. "I mean, well, his name is Hudson, but when I was seven, we were learning about the Hudson Bay in school, and since then I've called him that."

Oh my God, no wonder I never knew she had an Uncle Hudson.

"She's one for nicknames, this one," Hudson mentions. He doesn't take his eyes off of me, and I'm still not sure if my mouth is closed because my jaw dropped open somewhere in the last twenty seconds.

"I guess I only ever talk about my uncle who works in sports, never mentioned he was Hudson Arrows. That's how you recognize him, right?" April touches my arm as she enquires.

"Huh?" I glance to April and then straight back to the man who seems entertained by this situation.

"My uncle? He's the Winds football head coach. That's how you recognize him," she states.

My grandmother would most definitely be clutching her pearls if she knew I slept with my best friend's uncle/godfather who is walking her down the aisle, and apparently, he is also the famous football coach that every person who has a sliver of interest in Chicago sports has talked about at some point—except me. Because, apparently, I live under a rock, so I never realized who this man who made me see stars actually is.

Heat spreads through my body as I'm either blushing or getting swallowed by the predicament that I just found myself in.

Because this man is supposed to be walking my best friend down the aisle as a fill-in father, and she has no idea that he's my mystery man.

"Leave her alone, April. Something tells me your friend prefers sporting activities that involve ice." He tips his head slightly to the side before bringing the glass to his lips, and he sips his whiskey while trying to hide that damn sexy smirk.

Because his look tells me that tonight, he may just want me to squirm again.

HUDSON

Piper is standing before me, and yeah, I get my kicks out of her face turning slightly crimson. What are the chances that she and I were connected all along? Damn my niece and her love for nicknames, but this is a fucking fantastic twist.

Or at least, I'm enjoying this ride.

Piper, on the other hand, looks like she may combust. And I don't mind one bit.

"I'm going to check in on Jeff. Do you mind?" April asks us both.

Piper is quick to shake her head. "Of course not."

"Oh, don't you worry. I'm sure I can find something to talk to Piper about to keep her occupied." I throw on a cunning grin.

April smiles in appreciation before walking off, but my eyes remain on the woman who has been haunting my thoughts for weeks.

The breath of fresh air that I had for one night before she disappeared.

"This is not happening." Piper seems to be speaking to herself. Her chest is moving visibly up and down.

Stepping closer, I ensure that I'm close enough for the next few minutes of our conversation to be only between us.

"You know this coincidence is, well…" I can't pinpoint it, but a sound escapes me.

Her eyes dart up to my own. "April can't know about us."

"What? The part that we already met or the part that you love to sit on my face." I offer her a tight smile. I've never had qualms about taking people out of their comfort zone, that's what being a coach is all about.

Piper seems to grow a little agitated by my comment, proven by her sexy-as-hell death stare, but I don't care. After all, she left before dawn.

"You may find this humorous, but… damn it, I told her a few details about that night, not realizing who the hell you were. Oh no." She touches her mouth in a panic. "Exactly why she can't *ever* know."

Admittedly, it's going to be an awkward-as-fuck conversation with April one day if she does ever find out, but I can't help but point out the obvious.

My smirk stretches. "Ah, so you do remember that night in great detail and felt it was worthy of discussion."

Her eyes survey the room before she steps a smidgen closer to me. "That night wasn't… I mean, I don't normally do what I did."

I feel like she is trying to justify her actions, and I won't be having that. "You don't need an excuse, just own it. You are allowed to ride cock the way you do."

"Jesus," she curses. "Do you not have a filter?"

I chuckle under my breath. "Around you? No." That I'm honest about. "Besides, I don't exactly owe you manners after you left a cold spot on your side of the bed."

She sighs and looks away then back to me. "It was supposed to be one night. I thought it was easier that way. Sorry if I didn't follow procedure, but fucking a man old enough to be my father who turns out to be the godfather of my best friend doesn't exactly have a playbook…" Her last word drags for a second, and she seems to be considering something, then she laughs softly, and I'm adoring her all over again. "Now I get it. Foul. You chose the safe word."

I tip my glass to her. "Ding, ding."

She shakes her head but can't suppress a smile. "Clever."

"Is it?" There's doubt in my tone. "You didn't find me after. Could have easily done a quick search on the internet. Handsome guy, Hudson, killer tongue, Chicago, and I'm sure I would have been the first name to come up."

"And you could have done the same. Gorgeous, Piper, lingerie, Chicago, and I'm sure your world would have been blown," she chides but in a playful way.

This back-and-forth on my level is what has me drawn to her like a moth to a flame.

Taking a sip of my drink, I highlight a point. "You made the message clear that you wanted to forget that night."

Right? That's what it means when someone leaves without saying goodbye, or is it just how kids these days are playing the game?

"It's not that, it's just…" She chokes on her words. "I'd never done something like that. I thought it would be easier, and trust me when I say it wasn't something to forget."

That is exactly what I wanted to hear, because it means her departure has nothing to do with our connection.

Stepping dangerously closer to her, I lean in which causes the scent of peppermint to hit me. I know it's her shampoo because I had a fistful of her hair at one point that evening.

"It's okay. I didn't look for you, but that doesn't mean I

forgot. On the contrary, you're on repeat in my head far more than I would like to admit." I hear the heat in my tone, and as I step back, I see her slightly trembling as her lips part open.

But this conversation is going to have to take a pause because I see my sister waving at me from the other side of the room and motioning for me to come to her.

"Go grab yourself a drink, a very *dirty* martini, Piper. It may be a long night," I suggest before I walk away.

———

I ARRIVE at the corner where my sister—well, technically half-sister, but family is family—Catherine, watches the room. I can tell she's not herself tonight. That makes two of us.

I pass her a glass of wine that I picked up on my way over and hand it to her. Catherine is thirteen years my senior and works as a lawyer. Her mother was married to our father before they divorced, and he then married my mother. Despite our age difference, we're close enough, as proven by the fact she asked me to be April's godfather. My guess is that since Catherine and April have a different last name than me, theirs is Morris. These missing pieces of the puzzle made it possible for Piper and me to remain a mystery to one another. Especially as I've rarely seen April in the last few years.

"You think there are enough bruschetta plates?" my sister asks as she tugs on her earring. Ah, she's nervous that everything is right for the party.

"Trust me, I think people are more occupied with drinking tonight."

My sister snaps her eyes into my direction. "What's that supposed to mean?"

I shake off my comment and scan the room to find Piper, with no luck. "Nothing. Everyone is having a grand ole time."

"Should your publicist be worried?" She has a closed-mouth smile at her reference. "Use those NDA forms I gave you."

I shake my head. "Absolutely not." If I make a woman sign some form, then I'll never have a chance to find someone. "I'll take my chances, and besides, it just means that I need to be on good behavior at all times."

"Oh joy, you're thinking wisely." She mocks me the way siblings do. "You've done a damn good job at maintaining a positive image in the press on a personal level. That article on you giving kids a tour of the stadium was golden. In fact, you have been in the good books... which causes me to worry, because I know you, and you're my brother. Something must be up. You seem different." She waves a finger at me.

Looking to my sister, I can see she is hinting to something. "As in?"

She shrugs a shoulder before drinking her white wine. "All this wedding stuff getting to you? I mean April, and also Drew."

Now I proudly smile. My son is getting married. The son I didn't even know I had until a year ago, yet we've been trying to bond to make up for lost time. "I guess that's what happens when kids grow up."

"Except you never got to see him as a kid, you haven't experienced the childhood years. All of his firsts. Nor have you found a woman to tame you." She tips her head at me and flashes me knowing eyes.

Fair points on all counts.

Even though Catherine went into motherhood of her own will, she later found a man to call husband, but he only entered April's life when she was already an adult and they're not so close. Me? I've never been married, and as fun as the glorified bachelor title has been, I would like to shake it off at some point.

"Is this a therapy session? Anyways, Drew is sorry he isn't here, but it was just too much with his own wedding coming up next week."

Catherine places a hand on my shoulder. "It's okay, I understand, especially as it is a bit of a drive from Bluetop."

We both stand there in a moment of silence as we watch the room and people enjoying themselves. I don't see Piper, which has me slightly concerned she took off, but she must be here somewhere.

"How is Lake Spark?" Catherine asks.

My lake house is where I hide when the training schedule allows or in the off-season. I much prefer small-town life. In the city, I have no peace, and although I'm appreciative of the fans, it's nice to get away.

"I'm going to head there after Drew's wedding and stay up there through summer training." Quickly my eyes dart to the flash of peach fabric on a fine body. I spot Piper, and she sets an empty martini glass down on the bar before she walks in the direction of the ladies' rooms. "April explained my responsibilities at the wedding then introduced me to some of the bridal party, including Ginger who she sometimes mentioned, yet her actual name is Piper." I play it completely casual in hopes my sister doesn't question it.

"Oh yeah." She smiles. "Piper is such a good friend to her. She's a fashion designer, and they met a few years ago at some workshop. A bright girl. I'm not quite sure why she doesn't have a boyfriend, except she seems to be a bit of a workaholic. That reminds me, I need to talk to her about arranging a bridal shower."

"Right." I swipe a hand over my chin. Can't exactly ask more without Catherine becoming suspicious.

It also registers in my head that I'll be seeing more of Piper, whether she likes it or not. I've seen it with Drew, that weddings involve a lot of small events prior to the big day.

Lucky me.

"Sorry, I need to go chat with Jeff's parents," my sister mentions.

"Not a problem in the slightest."

It gives me an opportunity to find Piper.

————

I FEEL like a hunter as I walk out of the room. An almost animalistic sense hits me in relation to Piper, and I feel like I may know where to find her.

The moment that I reach the hall, my eyes scan for the ladies' room, and I head straight there. There is a joint lounge area between the men's and women's rooms, and I open the door. As I walk in, another man is leaving.

"Arrows!" he calls out. My guess is he's a friend of my niece's fiancé. "That was some playoff series. Maybe next year we'll use a little more offense." The young man smiles in good jest, but still, my return smile is tight.

"Thanks for the tip," I say, hiding my annoyance, and don't look over my shoulder as he leaves.

I take in my surroundings, and I'm thankful that it's quiet except for a member of staff in her forties standing by, ready to offer fresh towels or mints.

Clearing my throat, I throw on a look that is persuasive as much as it is charming as I catch the woman's glance.

Her face turns to surprise. "I know nothing about defense or offense, but my husband is a fan."

"Is that so?" Perfect. I reach out to grab a pack of matches sitting in a bowl on the counter. "By any chance is there a woman in there wearing a peach-colored dress with her hair soft around her face?"

"There is," she answers, intrigued.

I reach into my blazer, and I'm thankful that I have a pen. Pulling it out, I sign my name on the pack of matches then flip the box between my fingers to offer it to the lady. "For your husband."

Her mouth stretches into a wide grin as she slowly takes them. "Thank you."

"No problem." I hold my smile a little longer. "What would be the chances I could go in there?" I motion behind her to the women's room. "And let's say… nobody interrupts while I talk to that woman?" Her eyes bug out, and I realize what that must have sounded like. I'm quick to hold up my hand to calm her. "Relax. She's the maid of honor, and we need to plan a surprise for the future bride, and I wanted to hash out those details real quick."

The woman looks at me still skeptical, but after a few moments, she tips her nose up. "Okay. You have five minutes max, otherwise my boss may kill me."

I bring my hands together. "You are an angel. Thank you."

Without delay, I beeline it to the women's room, and as soon as I open the door, I close it and lock it.

In the mirror our eyes meet, and Piper's breath hitches, as she's startled. She must have been fixing her lipstick which may be useless if I have anything to say about it.

I walk a few strides in her direction, very well determined.

"Hudson, what in the wor—"

I grab her arm and spin her around until her ass rests

against the edge of the sink vanity. Her eyes slowly skim up my body until our gaze is locked which only builds the connection between us. I slowly let her arm go, but only because I already know her body and feel like she's comfortable enough to stay. Then I notice the hint of a smile on her lips, and I'm even more certain that this was the right move.

"Was your plan to hide away in here?" I grin.

She scoffs and looks away, only to return her line of sight to me with a warm smile breaking out on her lips. "If only that could work. But no, I just needed a few minutes to escape and come to grips with the fact that you're April's uncle and you are standing right in front of me."

"How did that go for you?"

Piper smirks at me and folds her arms up over her chest, almost as if she's settling in for a long conversation. "Admittedly… I may have searched your name on the internet for a good five minutes."

I tip my head to the side, and I step closer. "Honesty, I would be concerned if you didn't."

She taps her matching peach-colored nails on her crossed arms. "So, Hudson Arrows." She states my name in a tone that I recognize from her as thick with heat.

One step closer.

I'm already drowning in her presence.

"That would be me, Piper Dapper." I return the tone.

Piper's eyes survey me in curiosity to what I might do, and truthfully, all I want to do is run my hands all over her and play with that little bow tied under her breasts.

For a moment we both stand there, almost daring each other to make a move, until her lips part open again to speak. "We have ourselves a predicament."

A sound of doubt escapes me. "Depends on if you grabbed that martini or not?"

She scoffs a laugh, but sadly breaks away from our little bubble and walks to the middle of the room. "Made it a double, to be honest. I can't seem to wrap my head around this, except that April really can't know, especially not now, as it's her moment to shine."

I purse my lips before cutting to the chase. "Listen, we don't have time. My bribe with the lady outside only got us five minutes, and I think I've already used two to drink in the sight of you."

"So, what will you do with the other three minutes?" I see the smile she is trying to control.

"Convince you to see me again, away from here." I get to the point of the only thing that makes sense.

She smirks amusingly. "What makes you think I haven't started seeing someone else since our night?" I give her wide knowing eyes, and her smirk falters. "There hasn't been anyone."

My lips twitch from pride that I was her last. "Likewise. Now, about getting away from here…"

Piper's palm flies up to stop me. "The last thing we need is April seeing us leave together."

My hands go into my pockets as the corner of my lips curve up into a grin. "Love that you're thinking of what we could do tonight, but I meant something else."

Her eyes narrow, and her attention perks up. "You barely know me, Hudson."

"Debatable, as I know some aspects of you very well, but I want to talk to you some more."

Her throat cracks a sound, but no words come out. I take this as my opportunity to lead, and I take a few steps closer to touch the sides of her arms. Our touch ignites a feeling inside of me that I've rarely felt in my life. An inconsolable need to possess something, an infatuation that feels like it's leading me down a winding path.

"My son is getting married next week—"

"Son? The internet didn't tell me that."

I admire the view of my fingertips gliding along her bare arms as I say, "That's because I only found out about him last year, and I'm doing my damnedest to keep him out of the press."

"But you're telling me."

"Sometimes trust is instant with someone." That truth seems to hit both of us, as our eyes lock in recognition. "He's your age, in case you're wondering." That point I add because I know it riles her. Proven by the fact she swallows down a slight shock.

"Right." She looks away. "You're old enough to be my dad, yet I won't call you daddy in the bedroom." Her mouth gapes open when she realizes her mumble was loud and clear. Her eyes snap in my direction, and I can only laugh.

"We may need to circle back to that point one day. But anyway, as much as I would love for you to be my plus-one for his wedding, I doubt it's the time."

Piper tips her head to the side slightly in agreement.

"I have a house up on Lake Spark and tend to stay there when I don't need to be in the city. After the wedding next weekend, I plan on being there for a while. Come stay with me?"

Her eyes grow big. "What?"

I wrap an arm around her middle to pull her tight to me in an abrupt move. "You heard me."

Her hands land on my shoulders. "Like just escape the city with you?"

Arrogant, cocky, I don't care, but I'm not letting this go. "Call it a rendezvous, secret liaison, or my personal favorite heaven. Your choice of title but come stay with me and we can address a few things."

"Such as?" She raises her brows.

I squeeze her body against mine. I can't get enough of her. I want to go home tonight and debate showering because I want to keep her scent on me. That peppermint shampoo is a fucking aphrodisiac that has me desperate for more of her.

"Get to know one another, revisit what we already know." My eyes dip down to her body then back up.

"You're crazy." But her tone is only entertained.

"Tell me you're not curious," I challenge.

She licks her lips, trying not to let her smile break out, but I see her cheeks raise. "I think your five minutes are up."

I laugh at her avoidance of an answer. Instead, I run my hand along her back, sliding down until I land on the curve of her ass before sweeping my hand away. Stepping back, I grab a paper towel from the pile in the basket and pull out my pen from before. After jotting down my number, I hand it to her. I could easily input my number in her phone but writing it down with a pen from my suit is classic.

"Here. Call me when you make a decision."

Piper looks down at the contents in her hand with intrigue, which is promising, but I want to seal this deal. I glide my knuckles along her cheek to give her assurance. "If you remember what our night was like, then only imagine what the mornings could be."

With that, I walk away, leaving her to blush and stand in contemplation.

"Hudson," she calls out, and only when I look back at her does she continue. "Whatever my actions that morning may have implied, I don't regret it."

I simply nod, even more certain that this isn't our ending.

HUDSON

I knock a few times gently on the suite door before I check my tie, and when I hear Drew give the signal to come in, I open the door, already knowing I'm wearing my heart on my sleeve today.

The first thing I see is my son struggling with his tie as he looks in the mirror.

"I made it through the trenches and wanted to check in," I announce as I close the door behind me.

Drew is similar to me in so many ways. Those sharp blue eyes, I know they will drive his soon-to-be wife crazy, and I've been told by women that my eyes stand out. His shade of brown hair is much my own, minus the few sprinkles of gray that you can only see if you look closely. And that smile? A fucking Arrows hereditary trait that we can thank a distant ancestor for.

"How bad is it?" he wonders aloud as he grows frustrated with the fabric around his neck.

"I don't know about your fiancée because her sister-in-laws are keeping a tight ship on the area of the farm where they're getting her dressed. And Lucy's brothers? They look serious, double-checking everything is okay, and probably dying for a drink to calm the nerves."

My son is marrying the love of his life who happens to be his friends'—yes, plural—younger sister; she has three older brothers who all welcomed Drew into their family long before Lucy and Drew became a thing. They own a winery and farm called Olive Owl, so there was no escaping a wedding on site. It is convenient, as it is also an inn with a few rooms, such as the one we're in now.

"Let me help with that." I walk to Drew and take hold of his tie, and I can tell he is visibly nervous. Willingly he lets me take over, which is a surprise since he's more stubborn and independent normally. "Thanks for inviting the Arrows clan. My sister picked up my parents, and April will be here soon, she texted me from the car."

"You don't need to thank me. They're…"

We both raise a brow at one another and move past words. It's hard to say family when Drew has only met them a few times. Drew only came into my life a year ago when by chance I discovered an old high school fling had a baby. She's no longer in either of our lives, but it doesn't matter, as I ended up with the winning ticket. My son is the best, and we've grown close.

"And also, my neighbor and a few of the football guys," I add.

Drew shrugs a shoulder like it's nothing.

This tie is a pain in the ass; even I am struggling, but I won't relent, I have to get this right for his big day. "This will probably be one of the biggest days in your life, until one day you have a kid."

"Geez, no pressure or anything."

I snort a laugh. "That was a bad intro for my father-of-the-groom talk, wasn't it?"

"I mean… it was average." He smirks.

I take a deep breath. "Okay, let me try again. The moment I met you, I was lucky, not only that you are my son but that you have people in your life who care, and one of those people is Lucy. I've never known you without her in your life, and I feel like she is a part of you, and you do too. So today, you become her husband, and you'll probably make me a grandfather when I'm far too young and handsome to be one, but I wouldn't trade that for anything."

"Not even for a first-draft pick?"

I laugh. "No football talk here."

Holding the tie up, I assure him, "Come on, let's be honest. A tie isn't you, and Lucy won't mind if we ditch this thing. Your shirt under the blazer is fancy enough."

Drew contemplates and tips his head to the side. "Damn it, you're right."

I throw the tie to the side. "Points for effort, as I know you want to give her the perfect wedding."

We both walk to the room's small sitting area. Drew sits down, but I grab two bottles of water from the side and hand him one.

"You're going to be someone's husband," I point out the obvious.

He twists the cap off and looks at me. "I thought our sentimental talk was done."

I kick my feet up and land them on the coffee table. "Let the father of the groom go all in on this conversation, okay?" I smile to myself.

"Go on then."

"As much as I hate it, since I only just found you, but your wife is now number one. You love her like crazy and can't explain why you can't get enough of her. Every day you want to discover something little that is new and enjoy the things that remind you of why you love her. You are never ever to forget when she asks you to pick up something from the grocery store, and you gotta keep it exciting, I'll let your imagination run wild there."

Drew shakes his head. "And that's the cue to wrap up this conversation."

Probably for the best because my speech is running on instinct and what I assume it would be like.

I feel my phone vibrating in my inner breast pocket. Pulling it out, I check to see if it's Catherine, as she was driving my parents here. An unknown number.

"You can take that. We still have time to kill before I head downstairs."

I bring the phone to my ear. "I'll be quick. It could be my sister since sometimes her number comes up as unknown when she calls from the car." Drew nods, and I hit accept. "Hello."

"Hudson. Hi."

Her voice immediately causes me to straighten up to full attention, with my feet sliding off the table because I need the ground to stabilize me during this surprise. "Piper." My tone is steady, thank God.

Drew gives me a peculiar look with a hint of curiosity.

"Yeah… sorry, is this a bad time?" She continues.

I motion to Drew that I'll be right back in a minute or two and quickly head in the direction of the hall.

"No, it's okay. My son is getting married today, and we're just waiting for the big event."

"Oh, not a good time then—"

I cut in. "It's perfect timing, actually." I lean against the wall and focus on the sound of her voice and breath. A long exhale escapes me. "In truth, I could use a calming voice or more specifically the sound of *your* voice right about now."

"Why is that?" I can hear her smile.

"Being the father of the groom is a bit more daunting than I thought."

"I can only imagine."

"The bride's family I think have already used all the tissues in a five-mile radius, and I think I may be looking for one too," I admit.

She laughs. "Aw, you're a big softy."

"Whoa, I'm not saying that. It just seems like the bachelor party I arranged was a piece of cake compared to today." I adjust the phone against my ear.

She chortles a laugh. "I've never heard of the dad arranging a bachelor party."

I shrug a shoulder. "We have a different dynamic, Drew and me. I wanted to. His friends are the bride's brothers, so whoever arranged the party, it was going to be awkward. Besides, get your dirty mind out of the gutter, Piper. I kept it completely innocent with only one stripper instead of two." I'm joking about the last part, and I know by the sound of her laugh that she gets my sense of humor.

"You are something, Hudson Arrows." My name dances off her tongue, and it will keep me smiling for the next few minutes.

"Something good or something bad?"

It sounds like she is walking slowly. I can envision her playing with a plant or the pencils that she uses to design that lingerie of hers that I loved touching and peeling off with my teeth.

"As we now know, I know nothing about sports other than your coaching outfit from this one article I read looks kind of cozy, and the photos I've seen of you with models were not exactly encouraging, but you seem to have been flying solo for the last year, and I kind of have a problem…"

"Oh?" Something about her tone doesn't have me worried.

A sound escapes her lips. "The thing is, there is this guy who made this crazy offer, and it hasn't really left my mind. I can't even focus on work. But other than the lines of his body or the arrow tattooed on his skin, I think I should know more about him. He wants me to go up to his lake house, and he could be a crazy murderer for all I know."

Now I have to grin. "Something tells me that you had that theory once, then had an amazing night and still came out alive."

"I did, and as much as it was fun, I'm not sure sliding directly back into bed with you is smart. Besides the obvious complication, which is also a saving grace, because if April trusts you then I do, but I need to know more about you."

I think for a moment. "I still need to unravel all your secrets, Piper Dapper. I took a page from your book and looked online. You hide behind a cartoon vector as your profile pic and only post about fabrics and coffee on social media. I'm way too curious about you. You're different, and you have me laying my cards on the table. And as much as I would say my bed is your bed, I have guest rooms. It would be your choice if you use one or not."

She giggles. She actually giggles at what I thought was a gentlemanly offer.

"You're not giving me many reasons to run away, and I need to focus again. Your offer of visiting your lake house…" She's keeping me in suspense. "Will you send me the address?" It's her confirmation.

I'm thankful she can't see my confident smirk of satisfaction because I've been hoping for this.

"Yeah. I'll be there from tomorrow morning."

"Then I will see you sometime in the afternoon and maybe stay for a few days if, well… if it feels right."

I scoff a sound. *If it feels right.* She knows that answer. "Good… this was already going to be a great day, but it just got better."

We both hold on for a moment, just listening to our silence.

"I'm going to run so you can get back to your special day."

"Thanks. And Piper… why did you wait a week to call?" I propel myself off the wall to head back into Drew's groom suite.

She laughs. "Truthfully, I've dialed your number about ten times this week, but something inside me told me I should hit call today."

"Guess it's a sign then."

A sign for what, I'm not sure.

————

MY SON GIVES me a stern eye as I walk back into the room, admittedly more elated than before.

"Piper?" he enquires as he tosses his bottle of water to the side.

I scratch the back of my neck, debating what to say. Then again, the fun thing about our narrow age difference is that Drew and I hang out like we're buddies. Proven by our countless lunches, texts, and conversations.

"I've maybe met someone. I'm seeing where it goes," I say as casually as possible.

He looks at me, impressed. "Oh yeah?" A grin stretches on his mouth. "You didn't want to bring her as your plus-one?" He's entertained, I can tell by his tone and look.

"I want to focus on you today, and there may also be one minor detail…" My face must have an awkward expression.

His eyes encourage me to continue.

"She's slightly younger."

Drew laughs. "And? I wouldn't expect anything less. I mean, like what, five or ten years?"

"She's your age."

Now his grin is wide. "Why am I not surprised."

My hands go out as I shrug my shoulders. "Should I be offended?"

"No. Okay, well, that isn't a gamechanger."

I swipe a hand across my chin. "One more thing."

"Go on." Drew crosses his arms as he waits.

"I need you not to mention this… it's April's best friend."

Drew laughs deeply as he scratches his cheek in pure amusement. "Oh man, I needed this today. So, you're secretly seeing your niece's best friend? This is classic."

"Thanks. I'm happy my romantic endeavors can lighten your nerves," I say, sarcastic.

Drew fixes his collar and begins to walk in the direction of the door, indicating that it's time for the big event. "I hope it works out for you. You deserve someone."

"Oh yeah?"

Drew stops with his hand on the handle. "Yeah. I may have beaten you to the altar, but I think you were meant to be someone's other half for a long time now, you just haven't found that person. You're kind of one of those annoying people who loves with all their whole hearts."

"Again… is this a compliment?"

Or is it an unintentional flaunt, because yes, my son is getting everything I know I've always wanted but never had. The whole wife-and-family thing.

"It is. Lucy came back into my life when I found you.

Maybe Piper is coming into your life when your dear son is starting his own family. Timing is just a coincidence, huh, *Dad*."

Hit me in the heart.

There aren't many times that Drew has said dad to me, but now I think I may just need the rest of the tissues in a *ten*-mile radius.

But I will remain strong and fight back the tears stinging to break free. Nope. Will not cry, I'm going to fight those little droplets like the final play in the Superbowl.

I slap a hand on his shoulder. "Let's get you married, kid."

Blinking back a tear, I remind myself that today is about my son. Tomorrow is about Piper who finally agreed to join me on a much-needed escape.

6

PIPER

My heart is pattering at the speed of light, and I nervously tap my fingers on the steering wheel as I drive. I do my best to keep my eyes on the road, but it's hard not to look at the nature surrounding me. As I get closer to Lake Spark, the woods build up and the trees bring a tunnel of green over the road.

In normal circumstances, the scene may be calming, but I'm in an unusual situation.

"Come on, Piper, you agreed to this," I speak aloud to myself. A sort of pep talk for the twentieth time.

The only thing that can explain my decision is that sometimes in life you have a feeling so strong that it can't be ignored. Taking a chance on Hudson's offer is that very instance.

He hasn't left my mind, and that's a problem.

Then again, there was no chance of me forgetting Hudson Arrows from the moment he kissed me, and then the thought was only cemented when April introduced us. Which gives me a twinge of guilt. I texted her that I was going out of town for a few days for a fashion expo, because I have a sneaking suspicion she wouldn't be thrilled if she knew the truth.

I glance at my weekend bag on the backseat, and I feel my nerves building, with butterflies in my stomach running rampant as I approach the turn, according to the GPS.

This is crazy. So spontaneous, and damn, it could go so wrong.

What if we have nothing in common? Or it's only sex? Why am I even questioning this all, as if Hudson is a contender to become more?

I approach the security gate and stop. I reach my finger out to the intercom, and someone must have been watching for me on the other end because the gate opens before I get a chance to press the button.

It doesn't take long after entering for me to arrive at the end of the road, as it is a sort of cul-de-sac of three houses. Beautiful and big houses that are any architect's dream of modernity—well, two seem to be under construction, and the third I'll assume is Hudson's, and when I search for the number over the garage then I know I'm correct.

Parking on the driveway, I take one last big breath. "Here we go, Piper."

My heart rate is picking up, I feel it, but I open my door anyway, ready for this. Just as I slide out, Hudson emerges from the front door and walks down the path. He's in jeans with a white t-shirt, his chin has a little stubble, and his eyes catch the sunlight just right. But it's his widening grin as he approaches that has me weak in the knees.

"Welcome," he greets me. Yet he slows as he gets closer, perhaps waiting for my cue.

I tuck a strand of hair behind my ear. I'm in jeans and a light pink button-up shirt; it's cute, yet comfortable.

"Hi." I give him a half-smile because seeing him again is as exciting as it is daunting.

"I'm happy you made it here." One step closer.

My shoulder slants up toward my ears. "Afraid I would change my mind?"

He tips his head to the side. "Nah, you seem smart and know a good thing when you feel it. My question was more about how there have been a lot of foxes on the road. Even though it's afternoon, they still appear every now and then."

Is he for real? Or is he trying to lighten the mood? "Right, those killer foxes."

Next thing I know, I feel something hit my forehead, as if it dropped from the sky. I whimper in response and see a pinecone fall to the ground.

"Shit. Are you okay?" Hudson steps closer to me and touches my arm in concern.

I rub my forehead and try to smile through my embarrassment. "Wow, nature is trying to knock some sense into me."

Hudson's face floods with relief when he confirms that I'm okay. "I don't even know what to say because what are the odds? I mean, there is a pine tree above the driveway, but still… did it work? The knock-sense-into-you part?"

"Despite the foxes and dangerous pinecones, I still seem to be staying here." I rub the sap residue from my forehead.

Hudson chuckles under his breath. "Good. Do you have a bag that I can carry inside?"

Because I'm staying the night, multiple nights maybe.

"Yeah… let me grab it. It's not that heavy, I've got it."

I quickly open the backdoor of the car, take my bag, then close and lock my car. But I run into Hudson as I turn away from the door, and I feel like he may have done that on purpose.

Either way, the damage is done, and I inhale his cologne,

a subtle spicy scent. It takes me back to that night, reminding me that this man has seen me naked and has been inside of me.

Hudson hooks his finger and glides it along my cheek. "I'm happy you're here."

Warmth hits me in a wave and my adrenaline goes up a notch. I feel the tremble inside, but I'm not sure he notices. "I think me too, but I'm so out of my depth right now." I laugh nervously, and it causes him to smirk.

For a moment, our eyes catch, and I wish the power of his gaze would tell me to get back into that car, but it only encourages me to stay.

"Allow me, I'm a gentleman." He clucks the inside of his mouth as he takes my bag from my hand.

Now I have to grin. "Only some of the time." I raise my brows at him, and he appreciates my retort.

He studies my bag for a second. "Dancing lobsters. It's like your umbrella."

"It's a set. You remember my umbrella?" I'm surprised.

"I remember every second, Piper."

Swoon.

The one little ounce inside of me that might have thought Hudson was after a few nights of fun with a younger woman seem to be gone. He seems more invested than that.

Hudson steps aside and then leads the way. "You've come at a good time. The neighbor next door, Spencer, isn't around since he's remodeling. He's a baseball player, and it's game season anyhow. The other house just sold to a hockey player who is originally from around here. Last I checked, being in the sports industry wasn't a necessity to buy property here, but it makes for a good story, I guess."

"Sounds like you have quite the neighbors. Any of them single?" I can't help but tease him.

Hudson pauses as he opens the door to give me a flirty look. "You're already testing my restraint, huh?" His smile is strained.

"Nah, just being here is testing your restraint. It's when you show me the guest room that we may need to shackle you down."

Gone is the nervous woman from the car because something about this man makes me feel what I've always felt deep down but could never fully embrace. I am a confident person. I know I'm beautiful, and I know I have the ability to make someone like Hudson weak. In return, he is the type of thrill that may just challenge me.

"I don't regret my invitation, that's for sure. Shall we head to the kitchen for a drink?" he suggests, and I nod.

Taking in my surroundings, I'm impressed by the clean design and openness of the living and dining area. High ceilings with big windows wrap around the house, with a view out onto the lake. The deep blue water is surrounded by pine trees, and the long dock looks like a dream for the summer.

Hudson sets my bag on a chair before walking to the big fridge. "Maybe a soft drink? We can open a bottle of wine later, or if you want to explore the town, we could do that. I didn't make any dinner plans but thought I could cook."

"You cook?" I ask, impressed.

"Mostly grilling, but yes, I'm pretty decent in the kitchen. You?" He holds up two bottles, indicating for me to choose. Sparkling water or iced tea.

I point to the water. "I'm horrible in the kitchen except for breakfast food. I could eat breakfast for every meal."

He slides a glass with ice and the small bottle across the counter to me. "That's funny. You seemed to run when it involved breakfast with me."

"Fair point." I hold my glass up to him before I take a sip. "I don't think I need to explain myself again."

"You're right."

Setting my glass down, I realize that I haven't asked about yesterday yet. "How was the wedding?"

Hudson smiles with pride. "Perfect in every way. I didn't really get a chance to chat with April and subtly investigate you, I was too busy with father of the groom duties and talking with guests."

I love how he gushes over his responsibilities. "Tell me about your son."

"Drew is the best."

Hudson grabs his phone that was lying on the counter, and he comes to stand next to me, which causes our arms to graze and a spark to sizzle inside of me. Looking at the screen, I see a man who looks similar to Hudson with a woman who is clearly a bride in an embrace beside a haystack. He swipes his screen, then I see a photo of Hudson with Drew, and it melts my heart, as they are clearly happy and, by their looks, related.

"It seems like a lovely wedding. Very rustic, yet chic."

"The wine was top-notch too since Lucy, my daughter-in-law, her brothers own the Olive Owl label. Anyways, they're heading off on their honeymoon tomorrow. It was my gift to them, a trip around Europe." Hudson locks his phone screen and slides the device back into his pocket.

"I'm jealous. Italy is my favorite place, just sitting in a café drinking cappuccino, watching the world go by," I comment.

Hudson nudges my arm. "For coffee, we have a good spot in town."

"Wonderful." My smile fades, and I hesitate. "Can I ask, well, you mentioned that Drew is new to your life?"

His lips quirk then press together. "Yes. I found out a little over a year ago. An old friend of Drew's mother was dying and had a list of things she wanted to do before she died. One of those things was to tell me that Drew is mine. I had no idea. I was a teenager at the time, not from her area. We met at a party, and I never knew. After a little digging, it seemed that Drew was indeed mine. His mother didn't stay long in his life. He was raised by his stepdad who didn't stick around once he turned eighteen. Drew didn't get the life that I would have wanted for him."

I can sense a lot of feelings stir inside of Hudson about that. Instinct causes me to reach out and touch his arm to comfort him. "And now?"

"Couldn't be happier to have my son in my life. Just missed all the young years when he was growing up. He is the opposite of me in some ways, maybe a bit more intro-verted and not much for sports. He plays guitar and is good at carpentry, even made some of the shelves in my living room."

I squeeze his arm. "Makes his father proud too, I can see it with every word you say."

Hudson smiles to himself. "True. Now how about a tour?" he suggests.

"Sounds good."

For the next few minutes, he shows me around down-stairs, the at-home gym, and outside where there is a giant patio and an in-ground hot tub in the corner. It will be nice to sit out there in the morning with coffee and my design book. Color-wise, everything in the house screams bachelor, with neutral colors, except for a beautiful Native American rug hanging on the wall in Hudson's office—oh, and his hallway is decorated with a few of his old jerseys. We kept conversa-tion to the point, Hudson mostly explaining where things were.

But as we walk up each step leading upstairs, that feeling in my stomach returns. A swirl of anticipation and nerves. Maybe he picks up on it or perhaps he just doesn't want to make a big deal about it, but he doesn't show me his room. I thought for sure he would make a joke about it at least. Instead, he points out two guestrooms, and at the third room, he opens the door.

"This can be you." I follow him in, and he sets my bag on the bed. "Towels are in the bathroom over there behind the door in the corner. I guess maybe you want a few moments to freshen up before we head into town or go for a walk, whatever you want."

I notice he's avoiding eye contact. "Thanks. It's a beautiful room." I look around, and I do love the look of the white blankets with deep blue pillows. "I noticed you have a few rooms, so why this one?"

A droll smirk forms on his mouth, and his head lolls to the side as his eyes meet mine. "It's the farthest from my bedroom."

I feel my cheeks heat, and I try to hide my grin but fail, before I swallow and breathe in some composure. "You know, how about we just stay here tonight and open some wine and cook—or I watch you cook so I don't burn the house down."

"Sure. I'll meet you downstairs." Hudson turns to leave and makes it to the door where he stops, with his hand on the pane of the door, then turns back to me. "You know this is crazy for me too."

"So I make you do things you normally wouldn't do too?" I wonder, and I'm relieved that he also seems unsure about what's going to transpire.

He doesn't answer but instead scoffs, a hint of a smirk on his lips, before leaving me there to catch my breath.

———

AFTER CHECKING myself in the mirror, I return downstairs to find Hudson arranging cheese and crackers on a plate.

He glances up, and gosh, I don't think I will ever tire of his smile when he's happy to see me.

"White or red?"

I find a spot on the kitchen island. "Anything is okay, you decide."

Investigating the snack plate, and wow, the man knows how to prepare a charcuterie board.

"I was thinking maybe just steak and vegetables for dinner, but then I realized I don't know what you like." Hudson gets to work on uncorking a bottle of white.

"I'm pretty easy, I don't eat much pork, though." He gives me peculiar eyes, and I explain further. "My mom is Jewish and my dad Catholic, best of both worlds, but my mom won on what we ate in the house growing up."

He pours me a glass. "Ah, well, a wise man knows that the woman leads the way."

"Is that so?" I feel a coy smile stretch on my mouth, as I feel that he is insinuating me and where our day may lead.

Hudson offers me the glass, and he holds his own out to suggest a toast. "I'll cheers to that. You lead the way."

"I like the sound of that." I smile before clinking our glasses together, and I notice our eye contact is intense but in an electric way, which makes me thankful for the wine.

He indicates his head in the direction of the patio. "Some fresh air?"

"With that view, I don't think I'd ever say no."

I take the wine glasses and he takes the board of snacks, then we walk outside, taking a minute to get comfortable in the outdoor seating area, comfy lounge furniture with cloth pillows. He doesn't sit too far from me, but just enough to put my body on high alert. We angle our bodies toward one another as we hold onto the wine.

"So, you're Jewish?" he asks curiously.

"I guess. I was never raised in the religion. My grandmother, on the other hand, is a staunch follower, but more for the gossip from the temple than anything. Her family came from Hungary before the war, and my father's side is Dutch, but again, came long ago to the US. Dapper means brave in Dutch, actually."

"I like that. You are a brave person."

"How so?"

He has a sheepish look before he takes a quick sip of wine. "You took a chance on me."

I can't answer, only let our eyes hold. Maybe I will explain my reasoning when I've got more wine in me. Changing the subject quickly is my diversion.

"Actually, I got into design because of my grandmother. She comes from a family of seamstresses, and she became quite a big designer, back when department stores were king, and now, she's retired, with enough money to live a very good life. My parents were kind of the opposite, met during college, now work as doctors and volunteer time abroad, my brother too." I study Hudson for a second and watch how he listens intently. "If I can be honest, I think because of my grandmother, money and fame don't really faze me. Even though I could use my grandmother's name to get my foot through so many doors, I don't. So, I guess I'm not the typical woman you may have dated."

He looks at me oddly, and I realize what I suggested.

"Oh no, what I mean is, well… it's not right for me to make assumptions, but based on what I've seen online then… sorry." And I do it again, nervously ramble.

To my relief, Hudson chuckles and pops a cube of cheese into his mouth. "You're honest, I'll give you that. And for the sake of honesty, you're probably mostly right, but not as of late."

"Was there ever someone serious?" I wonder.

"Before coaching, I was on a vigorous schedule of training and games as a player. There were a few girlfriends here and there. But eventually, the schedule irritated them, or I could clearly see they were more interested in my fame. Then I turned coach, and my schedule became even more grueling, and life got chaotic. However, since my son came into my life, I've felt a need to slow down where I can. You?"

It's fair enough that he would ask me about my romantic life. I slide off the seat and walk a few steps with my wine to admire the view because I'm not ready to talk about that aspect of my life, not when Hudson could be the very opposite of what I've experienced.

"Such a great view. Why did you pick a house on Lake Spark?"

I feel him now standing and walking closer to me. "We train not far from here during the summer and for spring camps. During game season, I'm mostly living in hotels, and even though I have a place in the city, it isn't home. I even commute back here when schedule allows. I much prefer a small town on a lake, more solitude and calm. People just let me be, maybe because there are several people in the industry that live here, so the townsfolk are immune. My parents live in the western suburbs and will never move, even when I paid off their mortgage. It was the first thing I did when I got my contract money as an athlete. They're retired now. My mom was a teacher and my dad a plant manager. When I retire, I hope it is to here—and by the way, retirement for an athlete, even turned coach, is still young, in case you're concerned about my talk of retirement."

I turn to him with a fond look. "Sounds like a wonderful plan. I'm slightly jealous. I'm not much of a city person, although that's all I know."

"Well, then it's good that you're here. You'll get to enjoy the things that you like and experience something new." I notice a subtle tic of his jaw which means he is insinuating himself; it only causes me to smirk.

Again, we stand there, getting lost in each other's eyes. There's a pull we're both trying to fight, but we have our head in the game.

It takes a few beats before Hudson speaks. "Can I ask you a question?" His tone is almost serious.

I nervously drink from my wine. "Of course. I think questions will be our theme for the next few days," I attempt to joke.

He steps closer, and I gulp, anticipation rising. His fingertips land on my shoulder, and the best kind of tingle runs through my body. "What's the real reason you're here?"

I take a deep breath and remind myself that I'm a confident person who might as well be straightforward. "I guess I'll be blunt."

"Please. Your candor struck me from the very beginning," he presses.

"I want to figure out if you're the man who is the perfect fuck or the man who has the potential to be more."

If a man ever had a winning grin, then Hudson Arrows just displayed it.

He leans in, his lips brushing along my cheek up toward my ear where I feel the tingle of his stubbled chin.

"Baby, I know I can be both, and I have every intention of showing you."

7

HUDSON

The sound of the knife chopping zucchini against the cutting board fills the room, and I should be paying a little more attention to what I'm doing, but I enjoy looking at Piper watch me. Her eyes almost twinkle from where she's sitting at the kitchen island, sipping from her glass of wine.

"How's the view?" I ask then push the vegetables to the side.

She looks into her wine as she twists the base of the glass. "Can't complain. The apron was a nice surprise." The corners of her mouth hitch up as she says that.

Looking down, I admire my choice of apron too. *This butt deserves a good rub* is displayed on the apron, along with an outline of a cow.

"Thanks. I have a collection, and I'm not even sure how that happened. Matches some of your pajama lines, I guess, or at least your quirky lobster umbrella."

"Your aprons say a lot about you. You have an uplifting personality, you enjoy humor, and life for that matter. At least from what I can tell. You're laid back is my impression, considering the life you live."

"A fair assessment. Speaking of which, I will probably be up early in the morning. I like to work out, then I have a video meeting with team management first thing." I check on the meat that I seasoned earlier and will throw it on the grill for a few minutes.

"You stay in shape, that I can tell, and no, don't take it as an ego boost, I'm just stating the obvious."

"It's the Arrows gene. We reach adulthood then time freezes for about forty years." Amusement floods her face. "But seriously, I don't want to be like other coaches who bulk up in a bad way, I want to stay in shape. I'll be right back, just going to grill the steaks."

"I can set the table," she mentions, as if she knows where everything can be found.

"Okay. The remote for the fireplace is by the coffee table."

A few minutes later, we have food on the dining table and there is an orange ember across the sky to the west. I'm lucky my house sits on the south side of the lake, which means I get both sunsets and sunrises. But in this moment, the sunset with a crackling fire to the side sets the mood perfectly.

We both sit down, and she seems pleased with the steak that I place in front of her.

"Looks delicious," she compliments.

I top up her wine glass, then it dawns on me that I haven't had dinner here with a woman since I bought the place a few years ago. There is a first and last time for everything, and I can't shake the idea that Piper could be both.

She holds out her glass of now red wine to me. "A toast to your meat-marinating skills."

"Cheers."

We clink and then drink before both attacking our plates of food.

Piper clears her throat. "You know, my grandmother would point out the obvious about what I'm doing. I'm basically going back to what my ancestors did, which was to get acquainted with one another to see if they were a match before their parents would barter out the details of how many donkeys to exchange." She's only half serious.

"I'm sure you're worth at least three donkeys," I joke. "I'm positive she would be proud that you got to know my body first, to see if my cock is up to standard. Get to the important stuff first, you know."

She nearly sputters her drink out, then waves a finger at me. "Your humor somehow, unbeknownst to me, I get it."

"Hey, I'm doing my damnedest to be a gentleman here and not have you laid on the dining table so I can make you the entrée," I mention before taking in a decent sip of wine.

Piper purposely takes a big bite of her steak, with her mouth wrapping around the fork. "You have exquisite taste." Her reply is sultry, and I like the way she narrows her eyes at me.

I take hold of my wine glass only to realize that this may not be enough to keep me from leaning over and pulling her face into my hands to kiss her senseless. I'm attracted to this woman and so very curious about what I can unravel to get to know her more.

Thinking of a safe topic to discuss, my mind turns to work, only to remember that this temptress in front of me designs lingerie, and I'm envisioning it on her right now.

"Does your work also entail bikinis? We can go into the hot tub after dinner if you want." There's no point trying to avoid the million ways she could take that offer, so I sit comfortably in my seat, owning my question.

A smile plays on her lips. "Actually no, I don't design swimwear, and truthfully my focus is on pajamas that you wear around the house on a practical level. My lingerie line is not my main business, but admittedly, since our encounter that one night, I may have had a little… inspiration." She quickly takes her wine glass and downs a sip.

"I'm inspiration?" I must have a cheeky look.

"Maybe," she says, playing coy. "But seriously, I got into lingerie because feeling beautiful when you go to bed is important, it's your me time."

I stand up from the table, grabbing my wine glass in the process. "You're killing me, Piper." My grin doesn't fade. "We're going to need more wine."

She waves her hand and laughs. "Oh God, no, I'm already feeling tipsy, and I need to be sharp around you."

It's almost becoming insufferable, the light feeling dancing between us. Obvious flirtation and enjoyment.

I nearly growl to myself because I'm about to snap. Setting the empty bottle back down, I let my urge overcome me, and in a flash, I grab her wrists and pull her up and out of her chair, bringing her close, tight to my body.

My move startles her, yet her eyes are ablaze with excitement. Piper glances down to see my hands wrapped around her delicate wrists before her gaze returns to lock with my own.

"I'm going crazy not touching you," I say huskily. I'm dying to slam my mouth onto hers, but I won't. "Your smile every time you talk, I could stare at it all night. I'm completely fucked if you don't feel this attraction between us."

An almost sly grin forms on her mouth. "I would say so, considering I'm staying here for a few days."

"So you're not going to leave first thing?" I double check like it was even on the cards.

She gently shakes her head. "All indications are no. Depending if that pinecone incident turns out to be a concussion, but ya know." Her playing it cool is killing me as much as it calms me.

I loosen my grip and set her free, our tense embrace now dispersing into the air, but our eyes never break contact.

"Come on, Hudson, we have steak to finish and a hot tub to get into." She tilts her head in the direction of the table, even gently taking my hand and leading me back to my spot at a safe distance from her.

As we sit down and she grabs the bowl of salad, she highlights the obvious. "Hmm, I wonder if I packed a bathing suit, actually," she says doubtfully, bringing a finger to her chin. "I might have to go naked."

Damn, we lasted two seconds before she taunts me again, but that's what I enjoy about her, the banter, or the fact she isn't overwhelmed by me.

———

THE REST OF DINNER, we talked about food, and travel, and just kept the conversation easy. She helped clear the table, but I told her not to bother too much, as my cleaning lady will come tomorrow morning. Piper disappeared upstairs to get ready for the hot tub, and I quickly threw on my swim shorts, started the tub, and got in to keep warm.

Luck is on my side, as the stars are out, and a half moon hangs above us. My head perks in the direction of the house when I hear the door slide open, and every step that Piper makes in the thick bathrobe that I left in her room just ups the ante of whatever in the world will transpire tonight.

"You're curious about what I have on underneath, aren't you?" She grins almost shyly, yet she has no problem being direct.

I stand in the water to offer her my hand, even though the tub is built into the ground and there is a sturdy railing to my side. Piper flashes her eyes at me and slowly unties the robe while I bite my bottom lip, trying not to be extremely turned on. She keeps the robe closed as the tie hangs loose at her sides, and she pauses to draw the thrill out.

"The options are all in my favor, you know." Bikini, bra, naked... all possibilities I approve of.

"I'm well aware, Hudson Arrows." The way she's toying with me or the sound of my name on her lips is enough to make me want to get on my knees to beg her to let me worship her body all night.

Then she lets the robe slide off her shoulders and fall to a pool at her feet, leaving her standing before me in a dark bikini that does a half-ass job of keeping her large tits covered, but that's beside the point—this woman is a goddess.

She throws me an appreciative look and takes my hand as she steps into the water. I lean in to mumble against her hair.

"You're making the stars jealous."

She chortles a laugh. "Wow, you have some lines." Finding a seat across from me, we both sink into the water, submerging our bodies as much as we can. "I love this. Did the architect design this area?"

I lean back in the water to get comfortable. "Yeah, and we made sure that at night I can see between the two tall pines over there." I point behind her. "I thought about a pool. Maybe I will do it, but it's just that the lake is right here, and a pool in Illinois is only usable from May if we're lucky until early September. There's an old guy across the lake who swims every morning, even when it's cold. The only time he doesn't swim is when there's ice."

"Oh yeah? Swimming in cold water is all the rage these days. They say it stops the aging process and is great for your circulation. I can't handle cold, so I'll take a pass," Piper explains before she too exhales a relaxing breath and admires the sky.

"Me too. I prefer to stay warm."

After a moment, she turns away and rests her head against her crossed arms on the edge of the tub. "I could look at this all night."

Me too, but not the sky.

"There is something about the silence here. If you listen closely you might hear an owl somewhere."

She hums a sound as she finds her peaceful moment in my presence and looking at the stars.

"We have kind of avoided talking about April," she mentions but remains in her trance.

I run a hand through my hair and continue to watch Piper. "The good thing about being here is that we're in our own world, and we don't need to address it quite yet." Because truthfully, I know April, and she will not take this lightly, and my sister will never let me hear the end of it, but I think this whole dynamic is more complicated for Piper than it is for me.

"True. I can just get lost here." She half turns her body to look over her shoulder to study me, and the light in the water warms her face. "I spent five minutes upstairs debating what I'm going to do."

"Hopefully to me," I quip.

The corner of her mouth curves before her gentle eyes peer up at me. "This attraction between us scares me." She swims the small distance to sit next to me, allowing our arms to graze. "For the sake of transparency, because you were open with me earlier about your son and everything really... I'm used to being cautious, and I'm not a risk-taker in terms of guys, I play it safe."

I assume there is more to it than that, and I won't press until she is ready to talk about the reason why, but her words only confirm that I need to let her lead.

Her voice grows soft. "You are a lot of things that could make my life implode, but this trust I feel around you was instant, and I just want you to kiss me."

"Say no more."

I don't waste a second, and I slide my hand into her hair to bring her closer. My lips meet hers before I take more, and her lips are at my mercy.

Piper murmurs a sweet sound, and I dip my tongue into her mouth to get more. My mind becomes lust-filled, and I am captivated by the taste of her lips and the feeling of her arms looping around my neck. The water shifts around us as I slide her closer to me, inviting her to sit on my lap, and I love that she obliges.

Reangling my mouth, I cover her lips because I want to devour her. She has the ability to take over the atmosphere, and the overpowering desire to be inside of Piper has my mind stuck on the crossroads of lost and where to kiss her next.

We need to part for air, but I think I'm only able to breathe if I know I get to plant my lips back onto hers after.

Our foreheads touch as we take a moment to inhale, but it only takes a second for me to realize she's sitting on my lap, and I'm going to lose my composure any second.

Before I can warn her, her lips are back on mine and she's kissing me like I'm the prize she's been waiting for.

Her murmurs get lost as she deepens our kiss, and my

hands move to cradle her face between my palms. Admittedly, I like to lead and control, yet I've been patient all day, and I'll continue to be until she gives the sign. Just in this minute, I need her to know that I enjoy her... a lot.

"No understatement, I can't get enough of you and only you." My breath is heavy as I speak against her mouth before pressing my lips back to hers.

"I noticed," she mumbles as she softens our kiss and glances down.

My guy didn't get the memo to wait for Piper's cues, but it doesn't seem to bother Piper, proven by the fact she licks her lips and grins.

"He knows a good thing when he sees it," I remark.

But the moment our kiss breaks, she returns to sitting next to me and rests her head against my shoulder.

I have no idea what I'm doing except acting like a man besotted, which goes slightly against my persona of calm and assured. I have no qualms for this change, and I take the opportunity to interlace our fingers under the water as we both look up at the sky again.

"As damaging as your kissing skills are, I'm still sleeping in the guest room," Piper declares. I glance to my side with wide eyes, and she scoffs with a smile. "We get a touchdown for being attracted to each other, but I need to have a clear mind when it comes to you. Plus, that bed in the guest room looks ridiculously comfy."

I kiss the top of her head. "I'm too much of a gentleman to try and persuade you otherwise."

"Good. Now tell me about your views on pets..."

———

WE TALKED until our skin began to wrinkle from too much time in the water, but now I feel the night is about to come to a close as we walk up the stairs wrapped in towels.

Damn, I would love to offer Piper a shower in my room, but I'm okay waiting because I know it will be worth it.

Arriving at the top of the stairs, she pauses. "I believe I'm this way and you are that way." She points to my room.

I sigh and keep my disappointment buried. "That is sadly the layout of my house."

Her smile hasn't faded in the last hour. "I'll see you in the morning. Thank you for a lovely evening."

"No need to thank me. I wanted you here because you stir something inside of me that I can't seem to shake, nor would I want to."

Her doe eyes pierce me with fondness. "Night, Hudson."

I lean in to kiss her cheek when all I want to do is throw her over my shoulder and spank her ass, but she's the one play where I have to follow the rule book she set.

It doesn't mean I can't throw in a few words. My lips brush along her jawline. "Think of me when you touch yourself tonight, and I'll do the same."

"You're confident that's what I'll be doing?" She gently pushes me back with her fingertips so I can see her challenging and entertained look.

"Baby, I'll be imagining such wild things that you'll feel it from your room, and I remember your body, and the way you look right now tells me you are already hanging on tight when all you want is to let go."

Her mouth parts open and her face turns pink before her confident smirk comes back. "The question is if I'll be doing it with or without lingerie on. Goodnight." She stands up on the balls of her feet to give me a quick peck on the cheek.

I already wish that tomorrow would come faster.

8

PIPER

Walking into the kitchen, I feel like Hudson must have already been up for hours, as there is a half-filled pot of coffee. When I came down the stairs, I heard him talking in his office which was expected as he told me he would be up early.

It's nine in the morning, but it feels like I slept in. When I woke, I laid in bed recapping the last 24 hours and realizing how much I want this feeling that is moving inside of me. Maybe I shouldn't, but it's for my taking if I'm willing to take the chance.

I grab a mug that Hudson left out near the pot to pour myself a cup, then I breathe in the smell as I look out across the room to the windows and the lake. It looks like it will be a beautiful day.

"Morning," I hear in Hudson's deep timbre voice.

I look over my shoulder to see him walking into the kitchen wearing jeans and a dark t-shirt. Damn it, it only brings out his eyes more, and with the charcoal color, his skin looks a little tan.

"Good morning." I smile as he walks to me with determined eyes, and I know what he's going to do, what I want him to do.

He hums a sound as his fingers slide into my hair and our lips fuse together. It's the kind of smooth and sweet kiss that is by far better than coffee to wake me up.

"We're making progress... you're joining me for *morning* coffee," he teases as our mouths part.

I smile shyly at his reference. "I said I would be here in the morning, and I keep my word." I notice our hands have linked of their own accord as we stand here in the middle of the kitchen. "How was your morning?"

"I didn't wake you, did I? Had a bit of a tense meeting. One of my guys that we just drafted has an injury, and it could be a toss-up if he'll be better for summer training or not."

"Not a great way to start the day, no."

He tilts his head to the dining area. "Breakfast or want to head straight into Lake Spark to explore a little?"

"You haven't eaten yet?"

"No. I normally just have a shake and then I don't eat until around now."

"In that case, a little breakfast would be great."

He begins to move in the direction of the stove, but I yank his arm back so he doesn't get far. "Bran flakes and raisins are fine."

Hudson looks at me like I'm crazy. "So, no omelet? I need to make sure you have your Hudson protein intake this morning." He winks at me, and I playfully slap his arm.

I give him serious eyes, but my smile doesn't fade. "Let's keep it simple, we have enough complications as it is."

He taps his finger on my nose before he breaks free and grabs supplies. By the time we're sitting at the dining table and pouring cereal into our bowls, I realize that I'm perfectly relaxed around Hudson, almost as if I walked into his house like I've been here before. I blame it on our connection, the bond that I wasn't expecting when I walked into a bar all those weeks ago.

"You'll love Lake Spark. There is a surprise for you." He plays with the spoon in the bowl.

"Really?"

He flashes his eyes at me, clearly not willing to elaborate.

An obvious issue dawns on me. "Uhm, I need to ask…" I nervously pull my hair to the side over one shoulder. "I mean, won't people notice that we're walking around town together? Do we have to worry about, well… April finding out? The world for that matter, but I am more concerned about April."

Hudson leans back in the chair and presses his lips together before he blows out a breath. "No. Or at least not the locals. I guess I'll just scratch the whole kissing you senseless on Main Street idea, and I'm probably going to have to ditch holding your hand as we stock up on condoms at the store too." I hear the humor in his tone, which I do appreciate, but I give him a look and he turns serious. "I'll make sure we get a private table for lunch, but I can't make promises about privacy unless we decide that we will never leave this house while you're here, which I mean, could be a great option, but I would like to show you around."

"That sounds reasonable."

"Good. And don't worry about April, she's a big girl."

I look at him, astonished that he's so laid back about this. "You slept with her best friend; I'm sure she'll look at you completely the same come Arrows family Thanksgiving," I say sarcastically.

The corners of his mouth twist. "Lucky us, I'm not at Thanksgiving, as it's one of the most important game weeks

of the year for me. Besides, we happened, Piper, and considering we don't regret it, then we might as well own it." He
tilts his head slightly to the side. "Now, if you decide that you
want to trade down to some other guy, then yeah, it may be
awkward as fuck, but we know that won't happen."

His cocky confidence is oddly not a deterrent.

I cross my arms over my chest. "Why are you so certain?"

Hudson stands to head back to the kitchen like he forgot
something, and on his journey he stops and leans down to
whisper near my ear. "Because we haven't even started yet
and already it's promising."

———

WALKING along the main street of Lake Spark, it isn't busy.
It's clear the flowerpots are filled with newly planted flowers,
the flag flying above the hardware store is well taken care of,
and there is a café that smells delicious, plus a few little
stores and a barbershop. It all reminds me of a scene from a
classic movie.

"This is adorable, I love this." I admire the town as I let
Hudson lead us to wherever our destination is. "It would be a
perfect spot for a boutique over there." I point to an empty
shop.

"That place used to have some great tailored suits, but the
owner was pushing eighty-five and wanted to retire. Haven't
heard any of the latest gossip if he's willing to sell yet, as
rumor has it that his kids are arguing over the place. Is that
something you want? A boutique?"

"Eventually. For now, I have my online store and rent
some space to put the orders together, but the landlord
already let me know that he is most likely selling soon. My
grandmother always pushes for me to go bigger, but a

boutique is more my scale and pace," I explain as we continue to walk.

"Your instinct will lead you in the best direction."

Huh, that phrase hits me right. So simple, and I'm not sure why I haven't heard it before.

I notice we're stopping, and I assess the location, a candy store called Jolly Joe's. "What's this?" I have to laugh.

Hudson's hand is firm on the handle of the door he is about to open. "Your surprise."

"Really?" I'm beaming like a child because I'm curious.

We walk through the door and a little bell chimes. The store is a classic candy store, with jars and jars of different types of candy. It's open-plan, and it seems two stores broke down the wall to become one.

"You told me once you are a stand-in-the-candy-store type of woman."

Ah, yes, I did. The night we met.

"True." I touch his arm to insist he stay close, and I lean in to speak low. "But you know I'm not that young, right? I'm very legal and can't be bribed with candy."

Hudson roars a laugh and continues to grin wide as he guides me by the hand farther into the store which has an ice cream parlor set up as a 1950s diner. Then my eyes catch a display, and I know that it is the reason why he brought me here.

"Gingerbread," I gasp. There are entire families of gingerbread cookies and different gingerbread men in different themes... doctors, firemen...

Hudson moves to stand behind me, and he rests his hands on my shoulders. "Look to the left."

My eyes dart to the end and a wide smile takes over my face. "My goodness, you are a local hero." There is a gingerbread man with an iced jersey that says coach, and I realize it's Hudson.

"I've always loved gingerbread." I hear his sinister undertone.

Ignoring him, I'm too much in my element and walk closer to the cookies behind a glass display case. "You've been hiding this up your sleeve this whole time?"

This is quite a coincidence, considering my nickname and references. Mostly, I love that he brought me here. He put thought into it.

"Wait." He holds up his hand. "Is this our gamechanger?"

I can't help it, and I walk into his arms that naturally wrap around my middle. "No, but this is quite a surprise and may just be the highlight of our day."

His look warns me before he pulls me closer and runs his hand down to my behind since nobody is around. "Highlight of the day? Not a fucking chance."

————

I STOCKED up on a bag of cola gummies. Hudson wasn't impressed with my choice, as he went for licorice. In the end, we didn't buy any gingerbread. Turns out the owner is not actually called Joe but Pete, an older man who clearly runs the place for fun. He is also the swimmer in the lake every morning. Hudson spoke to him for a few minutes while I stayed to the side, not quite sure how to interact. What does one do in my position? My awkwardness didn't last long, as Hudson kept glancing at me with a wink or soft smile.

After that visit, we moved to the restaurant on the lake called Catch 22. As soon as we entered, the staff looked at Hudson like he's royalty, yet Hudson didn't seem to notice. Instead, he asked one of the waitresses how her daughter was and asked the bus boy who brought us water how college was going.

Despite the lunchtime hour, it wasn't too busy, but still we nabbed a table away from everyone outside on the deck.

"Is there anyone in this town whose name you don't know?" I ask, quite taken by the man in front of me.

Hudson places his menu to the side. "I'm nobody special. I may have money and name, but I eat and sleep just like everyone. If I'm treated differently, then I have no hope of trying to live a somewhat laid-back life. I only use my fortune when I need to."

"Such as?"

He takes a sip of his iced tea. "A nice house, and when I found out I might have a son, I made sure I had the best investigator and lawyer around. And you better believe that I made sure Drew has a top-notch honeymoon too. I wasn't allowed to contribute to the wedding, as my daughter-in-law's family went traditional."

"Good for you, Hudson, and you have excellent taste in location when it comes to real estate. I don't know why I haven't been out here before. April mentioned Lake Spark a few times."

"A lot of people from the city head up to Wisconsin or Lake Galena. I'm not complaining, though, it keeps this little corner of the state a secret paradise." He untucks his sunglasses from his shirt and throws them on over his eyes. "Have an idea of what you want to eat?"

I examine the menu. "Probably the chicken club sandwich with fries. I'll do an extra Pilates class when I'm back in the city."

"There is actually a Pilates and yoga studio in the hotel, Dizzy Duck, that's the name. In case you want to join a class for future reference, in case you ever decide you want to return." His voice dances, and I know he's testing the waters to see what I'm feeling.

"I will remember that." I close my menu and sit tall just as the waitress arrives to take our order.

By the time food arrives, I realize I've lost track of time because I'm enjoying every word that Hudson speaks. It's a calm feeling that I felt the moment I woke up, but now it's just more... confirming. I'm where I should be.

"I had a bad relationship," I admit out loud, and I'm not sure why it rolled off my tongue without thought.

Hudson immediately darts his gaze to me and takes his sunglasses off. "Don't we all at some point in our lives?"

I shrug and stare at the fork in my hand. "It's a little more than that. We were living together very briefly. Not many people know. I was young, foolish, and it wasn't meant to be. My grandmother refusing to have him come to Friday dinners should have been a sign. She didn't approve, and she's a good judge of character."

Hudson moves up and out of his chair to sit next to me, and he scooches the chair closer to me. He's quick to take my hand and weave our fingers together. "What happened?"

A disruption, that's what happened. Or at least it felt like it.

I feel a numb hole in my stomach from the thought. "Can we just leave it at that for now? But let's just say that because of it, I'm even more cautious of what people may think. Besides, I buried myself in my career afterward, so I've moved on."

"I won't press, but it doesn't matter what people think. For years, I was called a lot of things, when I played ball and now when I coach. Too good for some and not good enough for others, you can't make everyone happy." His thumb glides along my hand as we remain linked.

"I know, but I still struggle to believe that. Anyways, I thought I would mention it because for some reason it made sense to tell you. I wanted to tell you. But now I just want to enjoy the afternoon together."

He smiles softly before kissing the curve of my shoulder gently, not caring that my skin is covered by my summer dress. "I'm getting to know you piece by piece. Normally I'm an all-at-once kind of guy, but for you, I think I could wait until I find every piece of your puzzle."

That's what I needed to hear, and it only makes me nuzzle my nose with his, eager to get back to his house.

————

OVER LUNCH, we laughed and enjoyed our meal before we ordered another few rounds of soft drinks because the early summer afternoon is just too perfect. But after a few drinks, I desperately needed the ladies' room, so I went to freshen up while Hudson settled the bill.

Returning to the table, I see that Hudson is talking to a little boy who looks to be about twelve.

"Next year, I'm in seventh grade, and I'm going to join the team as a linebacker," the kid explains.

I set my sunglasses on my head as I watch Hudson sign a napkin. "You are going to love it, but just remember to have fun. It's more important to play as a team than score. If you're too focused on scoring, then you'll never become a better player."

"Okay. What about the Winds? Will they reach the championship this year?"

Hudson laughs as he hands over the napkin to the boy who is clearly a fan. "Maybe. Either way, we'll play better than Wisconsin…" It earns him a laugh. I don't know much about football, but I do know that the Riders are the bitter rivals.

Hudson's eyes catch my own, and he quickly turns his attention back to the boy. "I think you're going to do great with football if that's something you enjoy. I'll be too busy with football season, but I'll tell Coach Goodwin over at the middle school which day to bring the team to watch practice." He touches the boy's shoulder and stands.

The boy's smile is from ear to ear before he runs off.

I slowly step closer, feeling my heart melt a little. "A fan?"

"Yeah. I can't say no to a kid. He was having lunch with his grandparents inside." Hudson grabs his phone and wallet from the table to slide them into his back pocket. "Shall we head back?"

I nod slowly, and I know what question is about to burst out, but I couldn't control it if I tried. "You want more children one day?"

"Oh, we're onto this conversation already?" he teases me.

I poke a finger at him. "Funny."

"Yeah. I do. I never got to do the baby/raising-a-little-human thing. I missed out. But I also know that a baby wouldn't be a replacement for Drew. However, I'm very aware that at this rate I'll be a grandfather before I'm a dad to a baby."

"Okay," is all I manage to say and grab his arm to drag him toward the exit.

But I know why I asked it. We have an age difference and that can sometimes mean we want different things in life, and while I am in no rush for kids now, or at least I don't think I am, I want the option one day.

The drive back is quiet, but more so because the weather and scenery just make it the type of drive that is better when nothing is said. It's peaceful and in truth lets me clear my thoughts.

Because later when Hudson is opening a bottle of wine in the kitchen while I change upstairs, I decide exactly what I want this evening.

As I walk into the living room, Hudson nearly drops the full glass of expensive champagne in his hand as he sits on the sofa. His eyes grow hungry as he watches me, surveys me, drinks in the view of my maroon satin nightie that barely covers my ass, and the thin straps fall off my shoulders when I move in a certain way.

I'm straddling him before he can speak. I plant a finger against his lips so he doesn't let a word escape, and I take the glass from his hands, drink a quick sip, then set it on the side table next to the ice bucket that holds the bottle of champagne.

His eyes survey me up and down as he hisses a breath. "About time."

I don't get to speak because his mouth covers my own before I get the chance.

Which is kind of what I was expecting when I strolled into the living room, because I want Hudson Arrows to take me the way he did the night we met.

9

PIPER

"I packed for all occasions." I give him a sultry look and rest my hands against his firm shoulders.

"You are such a good girl, Piper," Hudson says huskily, and I hear desire laced in his tone. He pulls my body closer and ensures that I'm positioned over his now-hard member, which causes me to let a moan of approval escape my lips.

He runs his hands up my body, and the material of my nighty drags with them to reveal that I have on a matching thong. He tips his head to get a better view, and after his inspection, he whistles in approval.

"A *very* good girl."

Our mouths meet and the kiss is warm and slow, a confirmation that this is what we want. He presses his firm lips to mine, and his tongue delves inside of my mouth. This man has the ability to kiss my breath away; I'm not immune to that fact floating in my head.

I break the kiss and reach over to the bucket of ice on the side table, and my body position gives Hudson ample opportunity to slide the strap down my shoulder and brush his lips along my skin and collarbone. The movement causing a sensation to spread across my breasts and my nipples to peak.

Grabbing a piece of ice, I hold it up to show him. "I want that night again," I whisper and press the cold cube against my neck, gliding it down slowly in the direction of my breasts.

Hudson's chuckle is a devilish rumble, and he acts quickly, because next thing I know, he grips my hips and tosses me off his lap where I land on my back along the couch cushion. Before I can even settle, he's hovering over me with confident eyes.

He coaxes my thighs wider, and he settles his body between them.

"As much as I want to watch you touch yourself with an ice cube, I think you'll remember that you won't get a chance to lead, but points for effort, baby." He pins my wrists above my head and leans over me, taking the ice from between my fingers in his teeth.

I remember. How could I forget? There's a reason this man is a coach. He likes to demand and be in control, and he has a winning mindset which works in my favor.

His eyes meet my own for one last check, and I can only nibble my bottom lip because my entire body is on fire, and my back lifts off the sofa to give into the feeling of the cube against me.

The burn of the cold ice isn't going to be enough to unwind me. Instead, Hudson is causing me to writhe from a desire that makes my pussy clench and ache. With the ice visible between his teeth, he uses his hand to pull the fabric down to reveal my nipple, and he squeezes and pinches, but it's more a quick caress or warning.

Using his mouth, he begins at the base of my neck and glides the ice to my nipple and circles, leaving a wet trail. He gives attention to each hard bud then pulls back slightly, showing me the ice is still trapped between his teeth. He does this while he pulls my legs up toward the ceiling, resting my ankles against his shoulder and he slides my thong up and off my body.

The moment my underwear flies through the air, he is already bringing my feet back to the couch. Keeping my legs wide, he dives in eagerly, the ice hitting my clit in one swift move, and I whimper before my breathing grows labored.

I let out a gasp and comb my fingers through his hair, then tighten my grip to hold on. Looking down at him, I watch as he uses the ice with such skill, creating a pattern up and down on my pussy, only to land on my clit. He circles and circles, causing me to teeter toward an edge already arriving.

Hudson peers up at me because I know he likes to watch me, especially when he's holding my thighs to keep them parted.

"I'm almost there already," I warn him with a strained breath and my vision is hazy.

My statement grabs his attention because he abandons his efforts, brings his head up, but still holds me wide then spits out the cube onto the floor.

"I want you to come, but it has to be on my tongue. I love your taste; it lingers in my mouth for days." He nearly jumps off the couch before he picks me up and slings me over his shoulder.

"What are you doing?" I can hear the smile in my voice.

He walks in the direction of the stairs, spanking my ass in a playful manner, as my lingerie is in a mess around my waist. "No fucking way you're coming on my sofa. The first time in this house is going to be on my bed."

This man is in far too good of shape, as he's carrying me up the stairs like I'm a doll, and it's so fucking hot.

"But my first time coming in this house was last night," I correct him with a coy voice, reminding him I was alone in the guest room, knowing damn well that it's a tease and the truth.

He growls at my words as he walks into his room and sets me down in front of the bed. I take a second to take in my surroundings of a large room with windows wrapped around the corner to overlook the lake. The bed is big enough for four, and I'm taken back by the white linens with a soft green throw blanket and matching pillows.

But I'm snapped back into what is happening when I see Hudson eagerly getting his shirt off.

"As much as I want you against the window, we're going to deviate a little on the replay. On all fours, Piper. Middle of the bed," he orders as he swings his shirt to the side onto the floor, and he begins to work his jeans.

Doing as I'm told, I get onto the bed and glance over my shoulder. Hudson is now down to his boxer briefs, and when those come off, he touches his ready cock and inspects his view of me.

The sight of him makes me want to touch him, but he's pulling me to the edge of the bed on all fours and caresses my ass before sliding a finger between my folds.

"Soaking wet for me," he comments right before his mouth lands on my pussy.

"Oh fuck," I moan.

He's licking me from behind. "So good, so damn good," Hudson murmurs before he switches to a new pattern against my bundle of nerves, and he brings another finger inside of me.

My hands clench the sheets, and I'm already too wired from downstairs that it only takes a few more strokes and I'm at my cusp, shaking against his tongue and crying out in pure satisfaction.

But he doesn't let me rest, because he flips me like a pancake so I'm on my back, then he's over me in full command.

It's his eyes, however, that have me trapped at this moment. A momentary stillness as we both get a little lost in our reflection of lust and want.

He balances his weight on one arm, which enables the fingers on his other hand to sweep away some of my loose hair.

"You're beautiful but about ten times more so when you're naked on my bed about to let me take you deep." Hudson kisses my lips, at first a peck, then he takes his time kissing me like it matters.

And I think it does. Or maybe I hope it does.

I sink into the mattress and let his kiss carry me into another world. I wrap my legs around him which causes his cock to rub against my pussy and instantly twitch against my clit. It only makes me pull him closer against my body.

"Careful, I may just slide right into you because you're so ready," he warns as his lips brush along my cheek.

The idea causes my walls to pulse, eager for his words to be true.

I should be wiser right now, considering I'm not on birth control.

Reaching between us, I take hold of his cock and work from the base up in long smooth strokes. His eyes hood closed for a second before he rolls us so we're lying on our sides facing one another, offering him the opportunity to touch me again, which must have been his goal, as his fingers play with me.

"I can't control myself around you. You cast a magic spell or something. I'm going to take you the way you should be punished for making us wait a day, then I'm going to make you come the way you should when you're with me," he warns in a whisper.

"I don't even know what that means, but I need you inside of me." I roll my hips in waves, trying to get friction against his skin.

He scoffs a sexy-as-hell laugh before rolling off the bed. I peel off the scrap of satin dangling down my middle as Hudson grabs a condom.

But everything is happening so fast because before I get a chance to take a moment to breathe, he is back at the bed and guiding my body back to all fours, and his hand pushes my upper back down so my ass is in the air.

"Tell me if I get too rough," he reminds me.

I nod but say nothing, as the feeling of his fingers testing my entrance is a distraction, and the moment his tip enters me, I feel full again.

He hisses with pleasure as he works his way fully inside of me. "So tight."

Hudson goes deep and finds a rhythm, and when he's comfortable with his speed and pace, he grabs my arms and brings them behind my back to hold them down in a fold, and now I know what he means about fucking me for punishment.

My body surrenders to him, and I'm relying on Hudson to hang on. I have no use of my arms as they're held tight, and he drives in and out of me relentlessly. My breasts jiggle with every movement, and I couldn't stop my feral sounds if I tried.

"Deep and hard," he states.

I feel my lips curve into a smirk. That night when we met, he did the same, except I was pinned to a window during round one, rode him on top during round two, and the man had a thing for discovering my flexibility during round three.

And here we are now and he's fucking me as though I'm familiar, his, and he knows my limits. The funny thing is, he knows my body. There is a natural current between us where we are attuned to one another's needs and wants.

"Hudson," I nearly scream as he grunts when he's fully inside of me before he pulls out then goes back in.

"You're going to drive me insane." His breathing is heavy.

Hudson lets my arms go, but they don't move as he had held them in a bind and they need a moment to loosen. He spanks my ass then encourages me to lie on my back, but his eyes inform me that he's switching to his softer side.

He guides my body to scoot back until my head lands on a pillow, and he's over me, re-entering and bringing my knees up to my shoulders to take me deep. My hands come out to cradle his face and our eyes meet in a gaze.

Inside of me, he moves slower, allowing us time to soak up the moment.

"You make me want it all at once." His tone is missing his confident edge. I wonder if he means position or maybe… us.

This is the most insane notion of my life. It must take more than a night and a few good days to feel like the world turns differently.

I shake the notion from my head and plant my mouth on his, kissing him as he moves inside of me.

We nuzzle our noses and let our mouths explore down our necks as we move together with every thrust.

"I remember the way you took me. I want you in my

mouth again, I want to be on top of you and for you to fuck me, guiding me just the way you like it," I explain in a daze of lust.

It causes Hudson to half-grin, and he slides his hand to the back of my neck. "Next round. Right now, I need to do what I've wanted to do since you showed up at my house."

I feel my impending orgasm and reach between us, only to have my hand pushed away. Hudson's knowing grin reminds me that he will handle it, and I feel the imprint of his long finger pressing against my clit.

He moves slightly and brings my legs to one side as he reangles to take me in a spooning position, but I'm able to stare straight up into his eyes that haven't broken contact.

"It's okay, baby, let go," he murmurs as he continues to draw a line along my collarbone with his lips.

I can't take this anymore, and my hand touches my forehead as I pant and moan.

"That's it. All over my cock, show me how much you enjoy me inside of you. How good you take my cock. Come on, baby, I won't come until you're trembling."

His praise takes me over the edge, and I begin to shake and tighten around his length as I coo his name. He brings his hand to softly cradle my jaw. "That's it, just like that." He speaks against my skin, his warm breath adding to my sensory overload.

I cry out as my orgasm draws to a finish, panting, my entire body heavy. I feel dizzy and almost as if I might black out, and my body is his as Hudson moves of his own accord to get himself to the other side.

He joins our hands together against the mattress, and a slew of curses comes out of his mouth as his hips buck and still, reaching his freefall.

Hudson is careful not to crush me, but he collapses next

to me, keeping our bodies close and staying inside of me. He kisses the curve of my shoulder as we both lie in bliss.

We look at one another and chuckle in the backs of our throats before kissing really quick.

"There is more to come," he confirms.

10

HUDSON

Walking into my room, I see a beautiful angel sleeping in my bed. Naked, thoroughly fucked, and showered in the morning sunlight.

Sliding off my boxers and then crawling back into bed, I wrap Piper into my arms and tuck her head underneath my chin. I've already noticed on several occasions how she molds perfectly into my arms. She sleeps way too peacefully.

I slept deep, and admittedly, that isn't normally the case when there is someone else between the sheets. They either move too much, breathe too hard, or I just let them stay because it was routine.

Not with Piper.

I still woke early because that's just my internal clock, but Tuesdays are my quieter days, and I don't have anything on the training or meeting schedule today. Still, I went downstairs to make sure the coffee machine had enough beans for when we have breakfast later, then returned upstairs and stood on the balcony to catch the sunrise. I thought of waking Piper, but she needs her rest after last night, as we were at it until the early hours, and we will be doing a repeat later too if I have any influence on the matter.

She hums a sound, and I feel her shuffle in my hold. "Mmm, good morning." Her drowsy murmur is weakening me, I feel it.

My eyes dip down to see the line of her lips stretch, and she has an elated look, with her eyes fluttering open.

"Morning."

I should let us lie like this, but she's wiggling against me, pressing her body into mine, and her heated look informs me that her version of waking up isn't the sweet scene I attempted to create in my head.

"Piper." I chuckle softly before I roll us slightly until I'm on my back and her body is splayed on top of me.

She presses her finger against my lips. "Shh."

I don't protest, nor would I ever. The feeling of her hand wrapping around my cock, gripping and pumping to see if I'm ready to go, has me slipping into another world, one where I am equally relaxed yet have no patience.

I quickly slide my fingers between us, and I feel how she woke up ready. I attempt to reach to the side table, but it's hopeless, and Piper completes the task of grabbing the little square package.

I get my guy secure in record time, and when I feel her pussy wrap around my cock, we both moan in harmony.

She places popcorn kisses along my face as her forearms rest by my ears. Her body is flush on top of me, and my hands hold her hips in place as I thrust up into her.

We simmer in this position for a few minutes, using kisses instead of words until that turns into panting breaths.

By the time she is completely spent on top of me, I'm not sure leaving this bed is even in our cards for today.

I stroke her hair and kiss her forehead, mumbling against

her skin. "This is how every morning with you should be."

"I agree."

Energy must overcome her, as she rolls off me with the sheet tangled around her body. The color on her cheeks is my doing and a sense of pride roars inside of me.

"Shower then breakfast?" She seems wide awake now.

"Lead the way." I grin.

She yanks my arm and leads us to my bathroom. The shower is quick, but she takes the opportunity to caress my body, and I do the same to her. In no time, I'm out on the patio in cotton shorts and t-shirt, sitting on one of the lounge chairs, looking at the lake with mugs of coffee in my hands. I see Piper walking toward me in yoga pants and a tank top, and I realize this woman has me wrapped around her finger, and I'm not complaining.

Handing her the coffee, she comes to sit between my legs with her back to my stomach. Nice. I like this position too.

"I'll bring my sketch pad out here later if you don't mind."

"Not at all. I'll do some reading and we can call it a domesticated morning."

A lazy morning of breakfast, coffee, reading, and Piper sounds idyllic. We can do laid back, and I appreciate that she seems to enjoy the little things in life.

"This is perfect. The air is so clear and crisp. Not too cold or warm, and just looking at the lake and trees makes me feel so relaxed," she mentions before taking a sip of her coffee.

"Here I thought it was what transpired last night that did it," I retort.

She glances over her shoulder with a smirk then kisses me quickly on the mouth before resettling into our embrace. "You don't have coaching stuff this morning?"

"Nah, you somehow have impeccable timing and had

your way with me on the perfect night of the week. Tuesdays are the league's down day. For now, I'm free, but when the season starts then Tuesdays are my days to go over videos with the other coaches."

"When does game season start?"

"Well, we have summer training starting in a few weeks, then September to February is football season, and February depends on how good we are. Wow, you really know nothing about football, and you live in Chicago." I'm still astonished by this fact.

She shrugs. "I'm the exception."

"That you are." I purse my lips against the rim of the mug for a second. "Anyway, when it's season time, my schedule is crazy. Trainings, games, management meetings. We travel half the time. It kind of takes time to adjust if you're not used to it." I hear it in my voice that I'm throwing out testers to see if she can handle it.

"Sounds grueling." She sounds unenthused.

Oh, not what I was hoping to hear.

She continues, "I guess it just means you need someone waiting for you when you get home. And if I get to look at this view every day, then I may just volunteer for the job." Her tone is peppier.

I wrap my arms tighter around her, as her answer is good enough for now. "Listen, with summer training coming up, I won't be in the city, as the training facility isn't far from here. Will you come back?"

Piper moves to angle her body to look at me. There's a look that I can only describe as vulnerability on her face. "You want me to come back?"

"Have I done anything to you in the last 48 hours that says differently?"

She licks her lips. "You have been a perfect host. But

coming back… I have no clue what we're doing," she states.

"Getting to know one another. Not trying to run away from this chemistry between us Enjoying the view. The list goes on," I assure her.

The corner of her mouth tugs into a soft smile. Clearly, she likes my answer.

"Can we talk about the topic you kind of brushed under the rug?" she asks.

"Which is?" I take another sip of my coffee then set it to the side table.

"April."

I tip my nose up in recognition then sigh. "You know, I always tell my son that it's only complicated if you make it complicated. As I said, she's a big girl, but I think you're closer with my niece than I am with her. I love the kid, and I'm happy she asked me to walk her down the aisle, but I don't see her as much as I used to. I would like to think she would find the coincidence of our meeting charming."

Piper subtly shakes her head. "That's not April. Besides, I'm not sure what we would even tell her because I have no idea what we're doing, but not telling her seems like a lie too. There is no win, but I know she will be mortified when she learns you're the mystery guy, considering what I told her. I just don't want to take away from her moment of happiness with her engagement. Actually, I just don't want to lose a friend, and this could be a one-way ticket to that."

I lean back on the chair and take Piper with me. "Okay." I hear defeat in my tone.

"Okay?"

"You said it yourself that you're not sure what we're doing." There is a tinge of annoyance in my tone and not because of Piper, but at myself, because I don't have a clear answer either, other than I'm completely infatuated.

"This may implode one day, Hudson, but I don't want that to happen right now," she adds.

I blow out a breath. "I *maybe* see your point. By the way, my son kind of knows."

Piper immediately comes up to sitting and presses her hand against my chest. "What?!"

I laugh at her facial expression. "Drew isn't April. We have an unusual relationship, we talk about things, and when you decided to call me, he was there, so I explained."

"Which details?" She seems concerned.

"Who you are. But don't worry, he'll only tell his wife."

"You're crazy, Hudson." Now she seems entertained.

I take the mug of coffee from her hand so we have nothing blocking our ability to touch. "Listen, you're right, and we'll keep our secret... for now." I slide my fingers through her hair until I'm holding her head firmly in place. "As much as I love the idea of this place being our hideaway from the world, eventually, if this thing between us is something more, then it will come out."

And I hope she can handle that because I see something unrecognizable in her eyes.

"Tell me you'll come back next week?" I feel almost desperation inside of me. I need more of her.

She nuzzles her cheek against my wrist. "I think... I can make that happen."

"Can and want are two different things," I inform her.

The corner of her mouth curves. "I maybe shouldn't, but I can't seem to say no... I want it to happen."

That was the answer I needed, and I cover her lips with my own in a demanding kiss.

"I have a week then to decide what I'm going to do with you next time," I confirm just as I slide my hand up under the fabric of her shirt.

11

PIPER

Looking into my cup of tea, I dip the bag as I sit waiting at a table. I feel a smile threatening to stretch on my mouth as I recall in my head the last few days.

Gosh, Hudson does something to make me feel alive.

Every conversation is light, every joke a laugh, and he is one of those people who lives life without a care in the world. And he's asking me to come along for the ride.

That's what it is, right? Fun. That's what it should be, but I can't shake the feeling that Hudson Arrows is a lightning strike that hits deep inside of me.

The pure thought spreads warmth inside of me, and I smile to myself.

"Hey, Ginger," April greets me as she slides her purse onto the high-top table.

I gently shake my head to bring me back to the present. "Hey there, stranger."

"I ordered a gin and tonic when I came in. Why are you drinking tea?" She smiles in bewilderment as she adjusts her hair and sits on the stool.

Looking at my drink and then April, my mouth parts open but stalls. In truth, I'm drinking tea to ensure alcohol doesn't influence what I say to April. Already, I feel slightly sour in my stomach from my lies, and a few nerves float inside of me.

"Saving myself for my grandmother's dinner tomorrow. You know how she gets with serving wine," I explain half-heartedly.

April seems to accept that answer, and she thanks the waiter for bringing her drink. "How was Austin?" She sips from her lemon-slice-rimmed glass.

"Austin?"

"Yeah, you had that fashion expo thing. You went to Texas, no?"

Right, I did say that. "It was normal. Nothing exciting, just good to network. So, tell me about wedding planning." I'm quick to divert our topic.

April frowns. "Okay, I guess."

"What do you mean? Haven't you started to talk about venues or something?"

She shrugs and takes another drink. "Not really. Jeff has been busy this week."

I reach out to touch her hand. "That kind of conversation needs a lot of attention, so if he has been busy, then it's probably not the best time," I do my best to assure her. Squeezing her hand, I tell her something to make her smile. "I began to play around with a design for your dress. I forgot the sketches at my office, which by the way I'll need to move out of next month. The landlord confirmed it today."

"Yay for dress designs. Boo for office. What are you going to do?"

I bob my head side to side as I sink my shoulders and lean back. "I don't know. Something inside me says to wait it out and have my living room become a chaotic nightmare of boxes until I figure out a more concrete option. My grandmother has a storage unit in her building that she said I could borrow. I'm trying not to think about it."

"Did my lobster statue curse you?" She attempts to smile.

"Nah. He may still bring me good luck, but I don't see it yet."

April's eyes scan around the room and then she scoffs a laugh.

"What's so funny?"

"My uncle is on the TV."

My eyes snap in the direction of the flatscreen over the bar. When I arrived it was playing the sports channel... which now in retrospect shouldn't be surprising.

I can't look away. I can't hear what he's saying, but Hudson is sitting in an interview, with that winning grin that makes me want to melt. The screen bounces back and forth between him speaking and a replay of a football game.

"He always knows how to schmooze for the camera. I remember this documentary, a sort of history of Hudson Arrows becoming one of the best coaches of our time. They really missed out on interviewing me." I can hear her joke in the last sentence.

I study the screen more intently and realize the replay is of a younger Hudson playing football, before the blonde-haired interviewer asks another one of her questions, which causes Hudson to smile in this suave manner that makes me internally shake my head, amused. He's charming everyone.

But that just makes it even better because something I've learned about Hudson is that he is genuinely the kind of guy who wears his heart on his sleeve. It isn't for show.

"How come you never mentioned what he does?" I wonder aloud but can't tear my eyes away from the screen.

Partly because I don't think I will ever get bored of looking at Hudson.

"He's just my uncle, no different than me. Besides, you already know he's down to earth."

My eyes whip back into April's direction, with fear running to my heart. "I do?"

"Yeah. I mean, you spoke with him at my engagement party, right? What did you two talk about?" she innocently asks before playing with the lemon from her drink.

"You mean when you left to go speak with someone?" I hope that's what she means, and I'm relieved when she nods her head. "Oh, um, you know, nothing crazy. He asked about work and how I know you." I take another sip of tea to hide any unease that may show on my face.

Only a few minutes in and I realize that I'm a horrible liar.

"Well, I'm sure he didn't flash around the fact that he is the highest-paid coach in the league or that everyone is waiting for him to show up with a Mrs. Arrows any day now," she casually mentions.

I cough a little from unease. "Really?"

"I think so. He hasn't really dated in a while or at least since his son entered the picture. Plus, the rumor is my uncle Bay will get traded next season."

"Why is that?"

"Another team may sweep in with a better offer, that's what the public notion is. But I think he may actually trade in pro-ball for college ball because he wants a bit of a quieter life. He isn't a recluse by any means, but he likes to retreat to his lake house." April raises a finger. "I should totally ask if we can borrow his house one weekend for a bachelorette party. You would love his house. Well, I mean, his neighbor is a pain in the ass, but we can just go during baseball season to avoid him."

I try to evade her eyes and only awkwardly nod.

This is unbearable. I just want to scream that I've already seen his amazing house, and yes, I know that Hudson enjoys his own little world on Lake Spark.

"Hey, so while I was waiting, the table behind us had a bit of a bombshell conversation happening. Crazy, really. The one friend told her other friend that she hooked up with her dad. What does a person do in that situation?" A total made-up story, but I need to test the waters somehow.

April flashes me wide eyes. "Wow, I missed that? Damn. Could you imagine? I mean, total end of a friendship there. What a betrayal, right?"

My throat feels tighter. "Right." That was weak-sounding, I'm sure of it.

"What a way to start an evening. Wild. Speaking of dating, any news on mystery guy?"

"Oh, uhm. Yeah, total bust. I reached out and it's just not meant to be," I lie yet again, securing more points for the award of bad friend.

"Other fish in the sea, right?" She gives me a consoling look.

"Absolutely."

"Want to head to the flea market next weekend?"

I pull on my earring and think up an excuse. But half the truth is okay, or at least a start. "I can't. I'm going to be out of town."

"Again?"

"Yeah, heading out for a family weekend. My grand-mother mentioned something about some fancy hotel in Wisconsin with cheese and wine. Nobody says no to my grandmother."

"Sounds fun."

I feel like a horrible friend right now. April is sitting in front of me, oblivious, and I'm selfishly lying to her because I'm giving in to desire.

I look up at the television again and see a scoreboard comparing game wins between Hudson coaching the team and the former coach. The numbers don't interest me, but the picture of the man does.

In that moment, it's what I need to remind myself that I had a plan for good reason. I don't know yet how to explain this to April, and for the first time in years I want to enjoy being with a man before addressing the consequences, or maybe I'm hoping that the end result isn't a consequence at all but rather a choice.

And I can't seem to figure out why I'm ignoring the risks so blatantly. Probably, because I'm counting down the days until I see him again.

12

HUDSON

With a solid soundtrack from Live on full blast from the speaker in my car, I drive along the road back to my house. I'm in a good mood because Piper is visiting again. I texted her this morning to ask for any requests for our menu this weekend, as I was heading to the grocery store, and she said she wanted me to surprise her. It made my trip to the store a little harder but by no means impossible.

What has been impossible is controlling the excitement that's been filling my lungs since the last time I saw her. This is what's supposed to happen when you want to be with someone, right?

Well, I mean, I know something is different because every time I think of Piper and me escaping the world together, my mind runs to the idea that maybe one day she will be waiting in the second row to watch me coach a game, there to support me as the woman in my life. I would be lying if I said that spending more than a few weekends with Piper hasn't come up in my mind.

I'm thinking of a longer timeline.

Arriving back to my street and crossing through the security gate, I notice that my neighbor, Spencer, is here talking to his contractor. I haven't seen him since my son's wedding.

He nods his head at me in greeting.

Rolling down my window, I quickly call out, "I need to drop some stuff in the fridge but want to grab a drink in five minutes?"

Spencer grins and lifts his sunglasses off his eyes to rest on his short brown hair that has been lightened by the sun. "Deal. Plus, my house is a mess, so your place it is." A cheeky look spreads on his face before stern lines return on his face when he glances at his contractor.

I laugh to myself as I drive away because clearly construction on his place isn't going to plan. Spencer is an athlete, focused and strong-willed. The pressure of the team is on his shoulders, as he has the winning arm that the media focuses on at every game. So yeah, he can be a bit… stiff to some.

After I get my car in the garage and unpack the groceries, I grab two bottles of Matchbox beer because that stuff is perfect for a warm summer day. When I head out to the patio, it's just in time, as Spencer is rounding the corner.

"Lucky me, I get laid-back Spencer. I would hate to be your contractor right now." I offer him the bottle.

Spencer scoffs a laugh. "I'm going crazy. They are behind schedule yet again and telling me the indoor pool is the issue, and I told them to sort it out, as it's not negotiable."

We both sit on a few chairs in the mid-afternoon sun.

"What are you even doing back? It's baseball season."

"I have a mini-break between home games and figured I would check on my place since I'm eager to move back in. You know? Avoid the city, humans in particular."

I chuckle at his humor. "Well, I can understand that and

hope the house is ready soon because the noise some days makes me want to egg your house."

Spencer grins as he takes a sip. "I'm perfect neighbor quality."

I tip my bottle to him. "That you are."

"What's been happening? Heard from Drew?"

I shake my head. "No, he's on his honeymoon but should be back next week. Thanks again for coming out to his wedding, considering it's baseball season."

"No need to thank me, happy to have been there. Any plans this weekend? I can get you seats for my game. Our team PR loves that stuff."

"Can't. Have plans."

He raises his brows. "Plans? You say it with a ridiculous smile. What's going on?"

"Nothing."

"You're such a bad liar."

True. Lying isn't for me, which is exactly what I'm doing to my niece. However, I feel it is more delaying the truth and allowing the opportunity for this thing between Piper and me to be explored and built. To me, that isn't lying.

Looking at my watch, I know Piper will be here any moment.

"No fucking way." Spencer seems entertained.

My eyes snap up to see him grinning.

"Hudson Arrows has a woman in his life."

"What makes you say that?" I can't deny the look of contentment forming on my face.

Spencer sets his bottle to the side. "You're expecting someone, that I can tell."

"There is someone," I confirm.

His eyes widen. "Do tell."

"No, because there is nothing to confirm or deny."

He eyes me skeptically. "Really bad liar," he reiterates. "What, did you meet in a bar or something?"

I don't answer.

Spencer chuckles and takes my lack of response as an answer. He crosses his arms over his chest. "Wow. That sounds unlike you. I mean, you know a good bar or two, but I've never seen you pick up someone at a bar. She must be something if you took a play from my book."

I lean back in my chair. "Sometimes, someone comes along who makes you do things."

"Shit. I haven't really seen you like this. You look rejuvenated, and I mean you looked pretty fucking happy at the wedding but what father wouldn't at his son's wedding? How long has this been going on?"

I sigh because I could use an ear. "Not long. We kind of met, then didn't reconnect until a few weeks later. She somewhat runs her own timeline." I leave out the detail she is the one who left before I woke. As much as I don't love that minor detail, I'm at peace with it now, as the world conspired with us to ensure we met again.

"Does she? Or are you just completely smitten that you let her run the show?" Spencer challenges me.

I lick my lips before biting the corner of my mouth. "I know patience isn't your strong suit, but sometimes it pays off. Besides, so far it's working, I mean, she isn't running away."

"I just kind of assumed that you would be so persistent that the poor woman wouldn't know what hit her, or are you just waiting for the right moment to throw in that aspect?"

"Hey, I'm being persistent, just adding a gentle touch," I justify.

"Hope it works. Of all the people I know, you are the guy who should have a woman locked down because you're just meant for that stuff. You've been waiting for years to find someone and always put other people first. I mean, damn, since Drew entered your life, it's like…" He brings his hands up to an uneven level with one another to indicate priority. "Football, Drew."

"Move that football hand down a notch. My kid goes first," I correct him proudly.

Spencer does as I say before bringing one hand even lower. "Then Hudson putting himself first is here."

I sigh because maybe he's right. Except only until recently, because now I am completely putting myself higher on the scale. I want to be selfish, and Piper is the reason that feeling resonates inside of me.

"That may be changing," I tell him.

His hands fall down. "Fucking hope so."

"Why in the world are you talking like you are the authority on this?" Spencer is me maybe ten years ago. He has no interest in settling down with someone, and he has reasons for that too.

Spencer shrugs. "No clue, except I envision you with a woman who dotes on you and preferably bakes so I get a neighbor who brings me cookies."

"She isn't much of a baker or cook."

"Huh, what good is she to you then?" he jokes.

"She is a lot of things. Good things. My blood flows differently lately, that kind of good."

"Does mystery woman have a name?" He takes a sip from his bottle.

The sound of the sliding door to my patio opening draws our attention to Piper who hesitantly steps out, as she must have just arrived.

I'm quick to get up and walk to her. "Hey. I didn't hear my security app ping me."

As soon as I reach her and touch her shoulder, I notice she seems out of sorts.

"Yeah, there was a construction worker keeping the gate open so they could get a truck of cement through, and your front door was unlocked, so I just kind of rolled right in... Security fail," she quips as her eyes stay fixed on Spencer.

Ah, I realize we have an audience, and she is slightly uncomfortable.

"This is my neighbor, Spencer."

Spencer stands and walks to her with his hand out to greet her. "Hi there. Spencer Crews. You must be..." He's waiting for me to make an introduction.

"This... is Piper." I think for a second. "She's a friend of April's and..." I have no idea why I'm trying to hide this. I have no desire to, but I'm following Piper's cues.

"I came here to discuss..." Piper seems to be coming up with a story. "A bridal shower that I need to throw for April... here." She bites her bottom lip.

I rub a hand across my jaw while Spencer looks between us and snorts a laugh.

"Well, aren't you two obvious. You may want to come up with a better cover story." I notice Spencer is looking between Piper and me, studying us. A droll smile forms when his brain seems to connect the age difference, and he clearly approves.

I clear my throat before Spencer makes a joke because I know he will. "Spencer here plays baseball."

Piper looks between us, bewildered. "Okay."

I love that she is completely unaffected that a star athlete is in front of her.

"Piper isn't into sports. Your name means nothing to her," I explain to Spencer.

Spencer looks at her, impressed. "She's a keeper."

Piper politely smiles in response.

Spencer points a thumb at me. "Hope this one has enough stamina for you?" There it is. The age reference.

Piper chuckles under her breath but also blushes at the same time. "Perfectly in shape."

My neighbor flashes an overdone smile at her answer. "I'll leave you two alone. I need to head back to the city anyhow. Nice meeting you." He tips his head slightly with a little wave.

"Likewise."

"Good luck with your game this weekend," I call out as Spencer disappears.

I then turn my attention to Piper who I'm beyond happy is in front of me.

"I wasn't expecting anyone else but you," she mentions.

I wrap an arm around her middle and walk her over to my chair. "Relax. He's my neighbor, friend, and a pain in my ass sometimes. He won't tell anyone that you've come here to get your Hudson fix."

She gives me a tight smile, but all worries get thrown out the window when I sit down and pull her onto my lap, with her arms looping around my neck.

"Hudson fix? Is that what I'm calling it?" She has a cute-as-fuck curious look on her face.

"I don't care what you call it, just kiss me, because I've been starving for you for days." I lean in to capture her willing mouth.

Kissing her again brings back the feeling of being with her. Instinct has me believing that her in my arms is where she is supposed to be, because despite every angle that I've tried to look at it, with her I feel grounded.

She murmurs a sound of satisfaction before dragging her

lips along mine. "The entire drive here I couldn't stop smiling," she admits.

I retreat a little to allow myself to look at her face, and I run my fingers through her silky hair. "That's promising. I was worried we might need a pinecone to hit you on the head again to knock sense into you."

She nearly snorts out a laugh. "That was such a ridiculous moment."

"You're in luck that it didn't happen when I met you. Otherwise, I would have to include that detail in the how-we-met story."

She nuzzles into my neck, and I pick up on the fact she inhales deeply, as if she's taking in my scent. I don't call her out on it, instead relishing the thought that she is taking in this minute.

"Was there traffic?"

"A little. I mean, this weather is fantastic, so people seem to be escaping the city. It'll be nice to just sit out here all weekend, preferably while I watch you cook."

"You're just using me for my view," I joke and tickle her side.

She begins to wiggle, and in retrospect this move was a bad call because it's causing friction against my dick, and I wanted to romance her a little before I have my way with her.

Piper giggles until I stop, wrapping her tighter in my arms before we kiss to calm us down. A soothing kiss that feels as natural as the air I breathe.

She dips her tongue into my mouth, and I welcome her. I'll give her anything she asks for.

I cradle her cheek and swipe my thumb across her skin. "What am I going to do with you?"

"I don't know. I gave you a week to think about it, remember?" she reminds me with knowing eyes.

"Oh, don't you worry, that part I know. I mean, should I wine and dine you first or throw you over my shoulder and take you upstairs?" I ask her seriously.

Piper hops off my lap to stand and holds out her hand. "That's an easy decision."

I join her in standing, with the corners of my mouth twisting, as I want to smirk. "Oh yeah?"

"Uh-huh." Her voice turns sultry, and she grabs the fabric of my shirt to pull me to her. She steps closer and her lips come back to my ear to whisper, "To the kitchen, I'm starving."

Looking at her, I realize that she is dead serious, and as much as I hate that answer, I equally love it because I want to hear about her week and talk. Besides, when we go to my room today, then we sure as hell aren't leaving it until breakfast.

———

FOR DINNER, I kept it simple, with Halloumi with grilled red onion, asparagus, and a vinaigrette pasta, for which Piper fawned over me in amazement that I cook. We ate casually at the counter before grabbing a bottle of wine and headed out to the dock to catch the last of the evening sun before it sets. I even turned on the decorative lightbulbs that hang along the dock.

We sit opposite each other on a blanket with wine glasses. There is a very gentle breeze on this warm June evening. I hope we survive, as the mosquitos may get us, but the sound of the water lapping gently is a soothing backdrop.

"I know I need a boat here but maybe next season," I explain.

"I guess it would be nice." Piper's lips tilt into a smirk. "So, the other day I was with April at a bar…"

I'm not sure why I'm scared. It isn't because she mentions April, but I'm fairly confident that it's the thought of some guy Piper's age probably trying to pick her up that has me on edge.

I adjust my neck in discomfort but patiently wait for her to finish her sentence.

"You were on the TV in some documentary."

I chuckle in relief before taking a sip of my wine. "Oh yeah?"

"About your football career."

I recall a documentary I did two years ago when I signed with the Winds. "They still show that thing?" I look into my glass, but I feel Piper's eyes on me.

"Yep. Can't lie, I was intrigued. Anyway, April mentioned that there is a rumor that you might get traded or something."

I peer up, wondering if it's concern that is laced in her tone. I swear that I sense it. "Only rumor. My contract with the team is for two more seasons, and they're already negotiating with my agent for a renewal, but I said I won't give an answer until mid-season. Otherwise, the option of another team somewhere else is on the table."

"Oh." She quickly occupies herself with her wine.

I set my glass to the side and take her free hand in mine, interlinking our fingers and staring at our dancing hands. "You can't get rid of me that easily. I'm staying around. If it's another team, I'm thinking of leaving pro-ball and moving to college ball in Hollows which isn't far from here."

Her lips twitch, and I have my answer; somewhere inside her, she was worried.

"Wouldn't that be a step down?"

"Don't particularly care," I say honestly and let her hand go to lean back on my propped elbows. "In the coming years, I expect a change in rhythm. It's been a grind since I was eighteen. First in college ball, then pro, then coaching. A break or slower pace is just what I'm after. Fuck, my son will probably make me a grandfather soon."

"I hope you get what you want."

"I always do, Piper."

"I could use your confidence in career direction. With my lease ending on my office space, I need to hurry to outsource a few things and really make operations run smooth for my online store." All week we sent little messages to ask how each other was, and she mentioned her talk with the landlord. "I began to look into a few options, and now I know why my grandmother always recommends that I sign a contract with department stores, as they do the hard work. But I still think this is right for me, keeping it small-scale."

"It's only complicated if you make it that way."

She smiles at me. "Your philosophy, how can I forget."

"Take time and assess your risks, and maybe they're not risks at all." I'm referring to her business, but I think it's a front for really meaning me.

Piper contemplates for a few seconds. "You're right. I'm sure fresh lake air will give me some perspective, and possibly a trip to Jolly Joe's if we can swing it. I mean, town seems pretty packed which doesn't equate to staying under the radar."

I tilt my head and study her which only entertains me. "You mean for you and me? Are you worried someone might plaster us online? The good-looking coach and the hot-as-fuck lingerie designer?"

She looks away from me. "Something like that."

"Piper, if that happens, then I would be honored to be

linked to you, if that's what the millennials are calling it these days." I take another sip of my wine.

She points a finger at me. "That's because you, Hudson, don't care what people think."

"Nope. I don't." I survey her facial expression, and then it dawns on me that something about this runs deeper. "But you do care."

"I don't know what I think about people's opinions, to be honest."

I invite her to come into my arms. "Why is that?"

She crawls on her hands and knees before nestling into my chest. So innocent, but I'm already imagining what she's got on underneath her skirt. Piper is about to speak but hesitates. "The sun is about to set."

Clearly, she doesn't want to talk about the root of her thoughts, and I don't push. But I can't say that I'll do the same tomorrow.

Instead, I bring her with me as my back rests against the blanket.

"For someone who may or may not care what people think, you know you're in my arms on a lake, and anyone could sail on by while I make you come."

Her eyes shoot up to look at my face. "What?"

"All afternoon and evening you've kept me waiting to touch your soaking panties, but that ends right now."

13

PIPER

He kisses me, and it's as warm as the summer air. Hudson's hand roams down my body and then slides up my thigh, dragging the fabric of my skirt with it on the journey.

"You know how much damn control it's taken to be this fucking patient since you arrived?" He speaks against my lips before nipping the corner of my mouth.

I bite my bottom lip as I smile to myself and press my fingertips against his chest to allow me to see his face. He adjusts to lying on his side, but his hand doesn't leave my thigh.

"Want to take this back inside?" I ask.

"No, I don't." Hudson's tone is so matter-of-fact, and his eyes pierce me as the sunset casts an orange hue over his face. "The thing is, it'll be dark the moment that sun disappears over the pines, but I'm not going to wait. You were a good girl and came prepared by wearing a skirt to cover where I put my fingers, and I have every intention of making you come because I've smelled your arousal all afternoon."

His fingers inch closer to the line of my panties and I feel my breath catch. My nipples turn rock hard, and my clit swells from a desperate need for him to touch me.

"That's some statement there, Coach."

He growls into my neck and uses his teeth to grab hold of some skin in a playful manner. "I haven't heard you call me that yet, but I'm in favor of it."

I instantly reach my hand down to touch the bulge in his pants. "Let's go inside so I can taste you."

He tsks me just as his fingers curl around the fabric of my panties and pull them to the side. "I said here, Piper. Trust me, nobody will know, and later you can ride me, with your beautiful tits bouncing... Nah, scratch that, I want to see your latest creation."

My laugh turns to a hitched surprised whimper, and my head falls back because he's running his long finger along my pussy then circling my clit.

"Soaking wet." His finger enters me, and he pumps his hand. "I have every intention to lick you later, preferably while you sit on my face, lean over, and suck my cock, but we don't need to get into logistics now."

There it is. Hudson's ability to sound serious but always bring humor to the moment makes me smile.

"Whatever you say, Coach." My voice is breathy because another finger is inside of me, and his thumb gives attention to my little bud.

My body moves with his fingers, finding a rhythm, and I look down to see his hand moving under my skirt, and I part my thighs wider.

I moan as he picks up the pace, and I'm not sure if it's Hudson or the thrill of anyone being able to see this, but I feel that I'm on a cusp of an orgasm already.

"You are so fucking beautiful when you let go."

Our eyes are fixed as his hand and fingers work their

magic.

"Take me," I insist, and it surprises even me. But I'm about to burst because I feel my inhibitions letting go and my trust is literally in Hudson's hands. "Slide into me from behind." It'll look like we're cuddling.

He chuckles softly under his breath. "Impatient."

"I'm serious," I wail a plea, and I reach for the button of his pants. "I've been waiting for you all week too."

Hudson ignores my request and focuses on making me come. "You are something magnificent, and don't you worry, I plan on living inside of you tonight. But right now, come so we can enjoy this sunset."

I can't answer as I begin to unravel around his fingers, my entire body's senses heightened.

And when I finally succumb from my orgasm and his fingers leave me, he lifts my skirt slightly and tilts his head down to inspect. That smirk forms with pride before he covers me again and straightens my skirt.

While I recover my breath, I watch him taste his fingers, and I nearly pant again. Then when he gives me a bruising kiss, concern hits me that maybe we are more passionate than anything.

That thought scares me, because you can't build a relationship on passion alone.

But then he tenderly kisses me, with his palm cupping my face.

"See? Your name suits you. What I like about you Piper is that even if you hesitate, you are brave enough to try things. You just need the reminder that you are willing to try, and I mean with everything in life. Me, your work, me again, and if you want to attempt to cook dinner then I wouldn't say no."

I laugh, so ridiculously happy. "I think I'm only more willing to try things when I'm around you."

"That's called trust, and I'll be damned, but you also bring out a trusting side of me too. Now before you overthink it, lie with me and let's look at that damn sky."

The feeling of his arms wrapping around me erases any doubts.

———

"DID they seriously put a jellybean in your coffee instead of sugar?" I ask in awe as Hudson and I walk out of Jolly Joe's.

"Yep." Hudson proudly takes a sip of coffee.

Last night after staying a little longer out on the dock, we went upstairs. He was very pleased with my choice of a cotton-and-lace black nightie. It was one of my simple designs, but the material feels like heaven on your skin, and it easily falls off too. Rolling around in bed with Hudson was a wonderful way to spend a Friday night, even if I'm slightly sore today.

We slept in—well, to us, nine is sleeping in—got dressed and headed into town to beat the crowds.

I reach into the paper bag and take out a cinnamon roll from the bakery next door and bite into the sticky dough. "Yum! Wow, this is… what? I mean, is this magic?"

It's a damn good cinnamon roll, which people forget is not an easy thing to make. Any sign of dry dough and it's game over.

"Probably. Sometimes they have orange rolls and those things… Christ, I'm gone."

Hudson offers me his arm, and I accept without thought. Well, not entirely true, but I throw caution to the wind.

"We can hit up the farmers' market and pick out some stuff for dinner, then maybe go for a walk up in the state park," he suggests.

"Sounds perfect."

I look around and see that nobody is taking much notice of us. The occasional passerby says *good morning*, but people seem to do that for everyone here.

"I kind of hate myself for living in the city and not trying to live in a small town. But my friends and grandmother are there, and I'm not sure delivery logistics would be as good as same-day delivery in the city."

"Surely, I'm not that old and need to explain that modern advancement means they don't rely on a horse-drawn carriage to deliver mail here, right?"

I swat his arm with my hand. "Funny."

"I need to enjoy this peace before my schedule gets crazy," he mentions. "Coaching staff have meetings all next week since summer training starts in two weeks."

"And then you have to travel for football season," I add on. The thought has crossed my mind that the luxury of our time and place has a running clock.

"Give me your phone later and I'll add the security system app for my house so I don't need to be home when you visit," Hudson states as if it's nothing, and we continue to stroll down the sidewalk.

"What do you mean?" I feel my chest tightening.

"You can come and go as you please. My house is your house, right? That's the saying."

I stop and tug him back when he tries to continue to walk. "That's kind of... for you not crazy, but for me..."

His eyes squint and lines form on his forehead. "It isn't a big deal."

"It's..." I can't get the words out, but I want to tell him. "A step."

"It's practical," he counters and touches my arm like I'm being ridiculous.

I nod quickly. "You're right. I'm being silly." I begin to walk, but this time it's Hudson who reels me back in like a yo-yo.

"What's going on in that pretty little head of yours?"

I glance away then back to him. I feel my leg twitch because I'm debating telling him something I've barely told anyone, but damn, honesty with Hudson comes so easily.

"Remember how I said that I lived with an ex?"

"Yeah."

"It was only for two months, and it just isn't a great memory."

Maybe he hears sadness in my voice, but concern spreads across Hudson's face and his eyes scan the scene. The coffee that is only half-empty in his hand is quickly thrown into the nearby trash can so fast that I can't comprehend time, but all I know is Hudson's hands are on my face, with the pads of his thumbs rubbing my cheeks, every circle filled with care.

"What happened?"

"It's not a big deal. I mean, it's not tiny either. Let's just say that one day when I decided to explore other types of nightwear, Vince wasn't thrilled. As in he ripped up my entire book of sketches not thrilled."

Hudson steps closer. "Go on." He sounds like he may kill someone, and I haven't even finished the story.

"He threw the remainder of the book at me, missed, but still. I don't even remember all he said, but I decided that seeing my papers crumpled on the floor was enough. I wasn't going to stick around to find out if his temper could get worse."

"Shit." He pulls me into a hug.

I place my hand against his chest to push him back because I want to finish my story.

"It was a few years ago, and we had been dating for a

year, taking things slow, then suddenly when I lived with him, I saw a different side. I know my worth and moved out that night, and I decided that my focus would be on my career."

"Dapper, right? Brave you are," he whispers, and he doesn't blink, instead staring at me almost... in admiration.

I scoff a laugh. "Maybe. But Vince's parents, friends, our mutual friends, and everyone including the mailman didn't see it that way. He'd been deployed in the military before we met and maybe even blamed his experiences overseas for his outburst. Everyone felt I abandoned him in his hour of need. I was the one destroying his happiness after his military tour, they all said, and I was called plenty of things."

"Is that maybe why you're afraid of people's opinions?"

"Probably. And for whatever reason, your simple suggestion reminded me of living with someone, and then my mind went from one dot to the next, and here I am before you like a nutcase."

"Not at all. The exact opposite. You are fucking amazing, and I get it. I understand what you're saying."

I smile softly in appreciation.

"But I'm not him. You're safe, and I love your career choice, as long as nobody ever sees your late-night creations on you except me." His tone is assuring, yet he brings a comforting lightness to the topic. But his eyes grow dark with a protectiveness. "I'm not going to back away from my offer." His hands grip my shoulders to ensure I stay perfectly in front of him, and I can't escape. "Because in football we sometimes run with the ball. We go for it, run and run, don't toss it or pass it, we don't even blink an eye, we just see an opportunity and race to get the touchdown. You, Piper Dapper, are my rush. I couldn't stop this play even if I tried."

WE WALKED QUIETLY DOWN to the lake at the end of Main Street. There's a gazebo and a small park. There was a little food truck with coffee, and we got another one, which was more than half-decent brew. For the most part, we didn't say much, just enjoyed each other's presence and the summer air. By the time we were driving back to the house, my thoughts were running rapidly as we rode on the winding road, with the beautiful green trees blocking the sun.

The same journey that I've taken a few times now.

Several occasions.

And I know that indicates the obvious.

Which is exactly why I feel like a smile wants to break through. My daze is interrupted by the feeling of the car parking, and I see that we're back at Hudson's.

Getting out of the car, I circle around until I'm staring at Hudson, and we both stand in front of the path to the front door, looking at one another.

Hudson is quick to jump to the side and wave his arm when a pinecone falls near him. "That damn tree has got to go."

"You should call a tree person and see about cutting it down to use it for firewood."

"Good point. So, hot tub or bottle of wine?"

I take hold of his arm and pull him to me. "I was kind of thinking you could set up that app on my phone so I can walk into your house whenever I please." A confident look floods my face since I'm satisfied with my decision.

And I need that app too, as I have every intention of surprising him.

14

HUDSON

"This is so great that you stopped by," I say, slapping a hand on my son's shoulder as he walks beside me up the path to my front door.

Drew and Lucy were in the area to pick up an order for Drew's work, and Drew wanted to deliver a new creation for my house. Even though I had a hell of a day at summer training, I will always make time for him, especially since I haven't seen him since his wedding. When he called this afternoon, there was zero hesitation. We'll just order pizza and throw back a beer.

"Truthfully, I knew I would get a free meal out of this," he jokes. Lucy is in the car quickly finishing up a call.

Drew and I walk through the front door, and maybe I'm so buzzed by the happiness that Drew is here, but I miss the fact that someone is already present in my house.

And as we walk into the kitchen, my entire world shifts.

Piper turns around where she's standing in the middle of my kitchen. "I thought I would surprise y—"

"Piper, you're here."

And fucking rocking it in my old training jersey and heels.

Those pink shoes from the first night we met are on her feet, which contrasts with her legs covered in deep blue stockings because she is clearly matching with my jersey, which she tied just above her belly button, and it's paired with gorgeous deep blue lace panties.

It takes a few seconds of me admiring this view, because I've never seen such a perfect image knowing it belongs to me, before I realize what's happening.

Piper squeals.

Drew curses, "Oh shit."

And only then do I understand that my son just walked in on my girlfriend trying to surprise me in a sexy manner that absolutely will be rewarded later.

"Okay, so that whole 'come and go as you please' idea kind of took an unexpected turn. This is *not* how this was supposed to go." Piper explains, absolutely mortified, I can tell by the shade of red on her face, but she seems to be holding it together.

"Why are you two just standing here?" I hear my daughter-in-law call out from behind me as she arrives, oblivious. "What the..." Her tone changes when she registers the scene.

From the corner of my eye, I already see Drew awkwardly looking away, but I'm quick to storm forward and grab any cloth that is in sight that may help before standing before Piper as her human shield.

But I feel the grin on my face not fading. Is that bad?

"Oh my God. This. Is. Not. Happening." Piper is embarrassed as hell.

This scene is moving so fast that I'm praying my son and daughter-in-law may erase it from their minds.

"Points for effort," I mutter into Piper's ear as I hand her what I grabbed.

"What in the world am I going to do with a tea towel?" she gasps.

I look down at my hand and tilt my head slightly to the side. "Okay, won't cover much."

Looking over my shoulder, I see my son has turned around, but Lucy looks like she struck gold and stands there, elated, with her hand across her face doing a half-ass job of covering her view. "I mean, I can't even tell you how this just fed my inspiration with writing ideas."

"I mentioned she writes romance books, right?" I quickly clarify to Piper.

Piper gawks her eyes at me. "Maybe we can do the introductions when I have a little more on the coverage front?"

"Oh yeah, sure. Why don't we give you a few minutes and you can meet us out back?" I suggest, and I know I'm being far too calm about this.

Piper quickly nods and scoots sideways out of the kitchen.

I can't help myself and I watch her head in the direction of the stairs.

Wow, she is a beauty. But it is way more than that because she wanted to surprise me.

With summer training now in full swing, our ability to chat via text all day is limited, and unless I have a meeting in the city or she can drive out to Lake Spark, then our availability to be with one another is sparse. But she came out from the city during my busy week to be here waiting for me, and I love the idea of a woman waiting for me at home, even more, if it's Piper.

The clearing of a throat draws my attention back to my other guests.

"Coast is clear," I declare then turn my attention to Lucy and Drew.

"That's Piper?" Lucy asks with a wide grin.

"Yep. The one and only." I smile awkwardly. "What are the chances we can erase the last two minutes?"

"Zero. Fucking zero," Drew answers, one-toned. "It's stuck in my brain, and I think I may need therapy."

I comb my hand through my hair and blow out a breath. "Let's just order pizza."

———

WHILE LUCY and Drew get comfortable outside with drinks, I head back inside to find Piper. I make it to the stairs just as her feet hit the bottom step. She's in jeans and a tank top now, but it doesn't deter any attraction in the slightest. My hands land on each side of the banister to form a human gate because I don't want her to step any farther until we have a check-in.

"Piper," I begin.

"Can I just go hide?" Her facial expression is slightly deflated

I run my fingers along the skin of her cheek. "Nah. I wouldn't be able to focus knowing you're here. Besides, I want you to meet Drew."

"I'm sure with clothes on," she quips.

She tries to avoid my eyes, but I hook my finger under her chin to draw her sight back to my own. "I love the surprise. I mean, I feel so lucky that it will live rent-free in my head."

"I've probably traumatized everyone else."

I grin, because of all the things in the world, this is the least of our worries. I must be giving my carefree attitude away, as I feel that I'm smiling to myself.

"Oh my God, you get a complete rise out of this," Piper accuses me, with her eyes ablaze.

I bob my head side to side in contemplation, knowing she isn't wrong. I wrap my arms around her middle and pull her flush to me. "A little. You will find the humor in this one day."

She slaps my shoulder playfully. "How? I am so embarrassed, and I literally made the worst first impression."

"Only in your mind is it that way. Trust me, they're laid-back people, and besides, you're brave, so you can handle this."

"Hudson, I'm... sorry."

My face turns puzzled. "For what? Looking like a complete goddess in my favorite old jersey? Don't apologize." I glide my hands through her hair to cradle her head. "Now let me finally kiss you."

I plant my lips on hers and kiss her with what I hope is reassurance, and if I'm being true to myself, then this kiss is selfishness because I've missed her. I don't like the nights when she isn't here. And I just love kissing her soft lips that often taste of some vanilla lip balm, and any stolen moments that I can get with her are appreciated.

She murmurs a sound of delight as she pulls away from my kiss, clearly a tad calmer. "I needed that." An exhale accompanies her shoulders sinking down.

I kiss her forehead. "Come on, we have pizza and proper introductions to make. It shouldn't be a long night, as they plan to drive back tonight. They were in the area, and Drew made a wood shelf for me and wanted to drop it off. I also need to be at the training facility bright and early, so we won't be late."

"Okay." She takes the hand I offer because I won't let her

go. "Wait!" Piper pauses us for a second. "I'm meeting your son."

"And?"

Her eyes grow big and indicate that I need to catch up. "Kind of a big step, Hudson."

"Wasn't exactly planned, but I'm not complaining." I cluck the inside of my cheek because I don't see this as a big event.

Our train is moving, and I hope she gets on it.

I see the subtle hint of a smile form on her mouth, and it's my sign to yank her hand lightly to follow me. I feel her hand tighten in my own with every step closer to outside.

"Babe, you may need to loosen the grip. I need this hand for later," I mutter and smile at the same time as I see Drew and Lucy in our view.

Piper obeys, and I decide my hand is better on her lower back to ensure she doesn't run away.

The moment we step outside, all eyes are on us. Looking between everyone, I ruefully shake my head, as this doesn't need to be awkward.

"This is Piper. Piper, this is my son Drew and his wife Lucy."

Drew gives his signature fingers in the air for a little wave. "Hi." He uncomfortably half smiles.

"Hi." Piper's smile is tight.

"Nice to meet you." Lucy offers a warm smile.

"I'm sure this will go down as memorable," Piper says as she flops on an empty chair.

I have to grin to myself as I pick up the bottle of wine on the table to pour Piper a drink. "I think this is turning out to be a great evening."

"Ignore him. He takes joy from uncomfortable situations," Drew mentions before taking a sip from his beer bottle.

Lucy is quick to clarify. "I mean, there is nothing to feel uncomfortable about. I think it's awesome that we got to witness this, slightly out of the box on the introductions, but if you and Hudson are a long-term thing, then I can totally bug my husband that he walked in on his future stepmom who is his age half-naked." She grins, completely at ease.

What I love about my daughter-in-law is that her words are 100% genuine and not malicious in any way. I have to laugh, while Piper's face stays blank, and her eyes don't blink.

I walk to Piper and hand her the wine while looking over my shoulder to my daughter-in-law. "You know, Lucy, I always knew you would be a good addition to the family."

"Okay, I'm putting my foot down on both of you dragging this out," Drew states.

I sit next to Piper and intertwine our fingers. "Message received. Does the shelf fit on the wall?" He went to check when I ordered pizza.

"A perfect fit, the wood is the right shade too."

"Hand-carved by the greatest," I add. "By the way, did you have a look at the schedule of which games you want to come to?" I ask him.

He shrugs a shoulder. "Not yet. I'll get back to you later in the week"

Lucy turns to Piper. "My husband doesn't provide much data, but I love him anyway. He mentioned that you make pajamas, and well, what you were modeling earlier."

Piper seems to relax. "I do. I own Piper Ginger—"

"What!" Lucy's excitement is in full swing again. "I love those pajamas. So soft and cute. I got a pair with frogs with crowns on it."

Piper smiles brightly. "Oh yeah? I actually have a box of new designs in my car if you want another pair."

Lucy looks at me and winks. "I approve of this match."

"I'm positive I don't need your approval, but fine, I'll take it," I tell her. I can't help but look at Piper affectionately.

"Hudson mentioned you write romance." Piper attempts to keep the conversation flowing.

Lucy nods. "I do. So, apologies if I look at you two like you're a case study. How did you two meet?"

Piper nervously giggles. "Uhm, well, fun story really."

"She walked into a bar, and I bought her a drink. Kept it classic."

Piper glances at me, and I see a keenness to my answer.

"I had no idea who he was. A sort of mystery." Piper squeezes my fingers once.

"Well, mystery solved." Drew surprises me with his straight-forward reply, as normally he's one to stay neutral, but I sense something is on his mind.

Piper just continues on. "Hudson talks about you all the time. He showed me the pictures from your wedding, and they were lovely. Also, the pieces of furniture you made are beautiful." She touches my shoulder. "Hudson doesn't brag much, except when it comes to you. He is a proud dad for sure."

"Yeah, I'm getting used to it. Sometimes he can be a real pain in the ass, but he always means well," my son responds with a bit of humor. "Do you like Lake Spark?"

"Love it. I wish I had visited this place sooner; the town is so ridiculously over-the-top quaint, but it's perfect."

It's the last thing I hear Piper say as I get a notification that the pizza guy is at the security gate. I'm quick to excuse myself and go to collect the pizza. Returning a few minutes later, I see that the three of them managed to get on with the conversation without me. They're talking about how I need to get a boat for my dock when I arrive with the pizzas.

The rest of dinner is simple yet feels right. We talk about Drew and Lucy's honeymoon and their favorite stops in Europe. They gush about Italy, and Piper shares about her visit there. We discuss Bluetop where they live and Piper's grandmother. Conversation flows, and I didn't doubt that it would.

By the time it seems to be getting late, Lucy goes to freshen up, and I head to the kitchen with Drew while we carry plates inside, and Piper gathers things from outside.

Drew places the dishes in the sink. "She's... nice."

My head perks up, as I sense this is Drew wanting to have a conversation in private. It's his opening line. He leans against the sink, and I cross my arms as I rest against the opposite counter.

"Oh boy, I feel something coming."

"April still hasn't figured it out?" Drew asks, and it surprises me, as he's one to normally keep the peace.

Since Piper is here then I plan on talking to her about it. "No."

"And you know what you're doing? I mean, this is going somewhere, isn't it?"

My eyes grow wide. "Are you giving me a relationship talk? Have we actually reversed the roles?"

He shrugs a shoulder. "So what if I am?"

I smirk to myself that I find myself in this situation. "Just say it."

"You always wear your heart on your sleeve. I can see you like her a lot. Piper would be lucky, but is this all the same for her as it is you? Is she as invested?"

"Wow, you are going deep here. Do you have red flags or something that I'm not aware of?" I adjust my stance, and I do listen to him intently, because if my son has something to say then I will always listen.

"I don't know. I do like her, I just… don't want you to get hurt. You deserve… a lot."

My heart grows heavy, because in front of me is my son who every time I see, it feels like our relationship is getting stronger, and a twinge of sadness hits me, that I didn't get all the years until now with him.

"I hear you. I promise, I know what I'm doing."

Drew slowly nods. "Okay. Well, we should head out."

I grab the kitchen towel because I need to keep myself busy from the fact that I feel so lucky that he cares. "It's getting late. Are you sure you don't want to stay?"

He chuckles. "After what I witnessed earlier? Hell no. I'm not staying in this house tonight." He propels off the sink to walk out of the kitchen. "By the way, old guy, you do realize if you wait too long then the chance your future grandkid is older than your baby is quite high."

"First off, not old. Second, are you trying to make it a competition for who has a kid first? And thank you, by the way, for highlighting that fact." I shake my head at him before I pull him into a side hug.

Just then Piper comes into the kitchen. She exchanges goodbyes with Drew as she walks in and he walks out. I quickly stop her in her tracks by touching her arm.

"I'm going to walk them to their car then head upstairs for a shower. It's been a long day." My end-of-day shower is a sort of ritual to clear my mind.

"Sure. I'll finish up in here."

I squint an eye at her as she seems to be acting funny. "You were eavesdropping, weren't you?"

"Maybe," she admits.

"All parts or just the last part."

Her face turns cartoonish. "Maybe all parts."

I run my knuckle along her cheek as I smile. "That's okay. I'll see you upstairs."

The discussion will have to wait.

———

I STAND in the corner of my bedroom with a towel wrapped around my waist. Piper won't be able to see me unless she turns around, which is exactly what I want, and the moment Piper walks through the door, I initiate my plan.

"Don't turn around, Piper." My voice is firm.

She freezes in place, and I slowly walk to her from behind, a tie hanging from my hand.

I notice her body trembles when I stand at a breath's distance.

"Allow me," I say and bring the cloth over her head to blindfold her.

"This…" She gasps. "Is…"

I tie a knot. "A surprise. I know. The theme of the night clearly."

"Hudson," she softly purrs.

"Shh, baby. Good girls should be rewarded."

15

HUDSON

I circle around Piper, observing her like prey. I love how her mouth is partly open in curiosity. I hook my finger under her chin to tip her mouth up for easy access before I kiss her with warm intent, drawing in her breath, humming satisfaction.

Pulling away, I brush my thumb along her bottom lip. "You trust me, don't you?"

She swallows. "Fully. It's unexplainable."

I move my fingers to the edge of her tank top to slowly pull up the fabric. "What you did earlier could easily bring a man to his knees."

A smirk forms on her lips as I urge her arms up over her head to get the tank off. "Is that what you're going to do?"

I scoff a laugh. "No. But it is what *you* are going to do. As much as I loved your surprise, you are a bit of a naughty girl, so get on your knees, Piper."

Her lips part open and her tongue darts to the corner of her mouth. She is about to obey, but I tsk.

"Uh-uh, take those jeans off first." I tap the button above her zipper with my long finger.

Her breath is audible, and she moves to take action. I have to bite my lip when I see her in only a bra and the panties from earlier. The stockings she had on will have to make an appearance another day.

I toss my towel to the side and I'm naked, but she has no idea until I grab her hands and place them on my hips before she drops to her knees.

"The blindfold will be good for you. You'll be more sensitive to touch," I tell her.

"I like the sound of that." Her tone grows sultry.

I look down to see that her tongue is out of her mouth, ready to lap the head of my cock, and I tangle my hands into her hair to help guide her when the time comes.

Heat coils below my navel the moment her wet tongue begins to lick my length.

"Mmm, dessert," she whispers before licking droplets off my tip. "I want so much more." She takes me into her mouth, starting with a slow long stroke before working herself into a rhythm.

I want so much more too.

This woman knows how to make me feel good. She alternates between using her hand and mouth. It's a talent she has, and I feel like my eyes may already be rolling to the back of my head, but I want to enjoy a little more of her watery mouth taking me in until I hit the back of her throat.

I'm a barbarian maybe because I like her lips swollen and the way she sounds when she moans as she pulls my hips closer to her. Piper is a determined woman in the bedroom; her confidence comes into full swing when sex is involved.

We're having a moment, and I'm not going to let us go too fast.

I grab hold of her shoulders. "Come here, baby."

She returns to standing and wipes the back of her hand

along her mouth. "Hudson, give me more." She's nearly pouting.

I walk us back to the edge of my bed, and I sit down, yanking her down until she's over my knee with her lace-covered ass in full view.

Piper glances over her shoulder even though she can't see. "I've had this fantasy going in my head for a long time now." Her grin brings a light-heartedness to our intimate moment that I appreciate.

"Like this? You deserve it." My palm lands on the flesh of her ass and the sound of the spank fills the room.

She whimpers in delight, and her behind goes pert and up, as if she's offering me more. I run my hand along her spine in a soothing line. I love wandering all over her body.

"I like this set. Another original?"

Piper glances over her shoulder again, and even though I can't see her eyes, her face tells me I'm crazy for asking the question when I clearly know the answer. "Always. You're my inspiration, Coach Arrows."

I unsnap the clasp of the bra. "I love when you talk dirty," I tease because she knows what hearing her say that does to me.

In a swift move, I wrap my arms around her and toss her onto the bed. "On your back and your legs wide." My hands coax her thighs open, and she plants her feet onto the mattress. Her body is already writhing in anticipation. "For-give me, but these panties have to go, and I may rip them in the process." I don't think twice, and I slide them up and off her legs in a gruff movement.

"I may accept the apology."

I chuckle as I eye her glistening pussy. "Oh, you will. I see you've been waiting for me."

"For days," she gasps.

I use my tongue to explore her pussy, my instant addiction kicking in.

"Mmhmm, right there." Her hand touches the top of my head.

I'm not going to go gently. I want to drive her to insanity and leave her begging. In fact, I will only let her come once tonight, because I'm selfish and it can only be while I'm buried deep inside of her.

But she doesn't need to know that plan quite yet.

I work at her with my fingers and tongue. Her thighs part wider from instinct, and I hold one down while my other hand reaches along her body and settles between her breasts and next to her heart. I want to keep her firm to the mattress and under my spell.

Peering up, I see Piper licking her lips, and her nipples are pebbled, ready for attention too.

"Definitely more sensitive." Her breath is ragged. "Everything is more sensitive." She takes hold of my hand to hold it securely against the one place of her body that I'm not sure I have any control over – her heart.

I suck and lick until I feel her getting close. I know her cues by now, and just as she begins to hit the peak of the mountain, I stop and kiss up her body.

"Not yet." I tug on her nipple with my teeth and love the feeling of her legs wrapping around my waist, the tip of my cock sliding along her slickness. "I'm going to bury myself so deep inside of you." I drag my lips along her collarbone before taking the other nipple.

"Take this blindfold off me. I need to see you."

"Why? Because you missed me and came all the way here to surprise me?" I look at her face and wonder what she's thinking.

Her expression is serious. "Exactly that."

The air in the room nearly evaporates because the sincerity in her tone stops us in our tracks. It's no longer fun and games, she feels something too.

I lean on my side and untie the blindfold, and it falls low. Her beautiful blue eyes slowly flick open and blink several times before a smile grows on her mouth.

Looking down at her, our eyes lock, and I don't dare look anywhere else. "Hey there, beautiful."

She drapes her leg over my hip and pushes me back until she's on top of me and I'm lying on my back. "Hi there." She leans down to plant a kiss on my lips.

But I like her under me, and I roll us over which causes Piper to giggle. "Tell me I get a raincheck on that whole outfit from earlier?" I ask.

"Sure. I'll remember to pack it next time."

"Fuck that. You can have a damn drawer here." I reach my fingers between us to toy with her again.

Her eyes hood closed then open. "Why do you say things that don't make me run away when they should?"

"Because it feels right to you. I leave that to fate." I speak against the skin of her neck because my lips need to be on her, anywhere, just her.

The feeling of her fingernails gliding along my back is subtle, but I enjoy when she does it. There isn't an inch of our bodies getting ignored.

She squirms underneath me and the tip of my cock is dangerously close to her opening, and I should take this opportunity to grab a condom, but her eyes have me kind of lost and we are simmering in a moment together.

Our relationship has been evolving throughout the last few weeks and months, and this is our moment of confirmation.

"It does feel right. I'm a little scared, but even when temporarily blind, I see you," Piper whispers.

I give her a quick kiss. My entire body wants to mold into her as I slide my lips down the curve of her shoulder. "You were waiting for me."

She hums in response as she rubs her pussy along my cock.

"Wait."

"It's okay," she whispers. "Please, just..."

I cover her mouth with my own, and I'm diving in even deeper both literally and figuratively with what I feel for her.

My eyes close as I feel her warm pussy envelope around my cock, and her body curves into me as we both moan together.

It's in that moment of entwined bodies that I realize what it is that has me completely at the grace of this woman when my plan was to have her at my mercy.

But I'll show her now and explain later.

———

PIPER RESTS her head against my chest, and I pull the blanket over us.

"Your hair smells like peppermint."

She giggles under her breath. "Probably because my shampoo has mint in it."

"It's damn distracting. It's a scent that keeps me alert."

"My apologies, I'll be sure to find a shampoo that puts you to sleep," she says, sarcastically.

I squeeze her close against me. "It wouldn't matter, I have my guard down around you anyways. It's just that the mint reminds me to think clearer."

Piper looks up at me with a brow raised, resting her chin against my pecs. "Penny for your thoughts, Hudson?"

"I couldn't have asked for a better night. I'm happy you met Drew and Lucy, and you only reaffirmed my thought that you are capable of surprising me."

Piper kisses quickly against my chest before moving to straddle me, her hair a wild mess. She clasps our hands together and rests them on each side of our joined bodies.

"He is right, you know. You should be careful." She's insinuating what she overheard earlier.

"Should I?" I challenge her. "Here's the thing, Piper. I've never been against the idea of relationships or love or walking into the sunset forever. I know I want it. I just didn't find someone who came anywhere close to being my other half. Until you walked into my life with a fucking dancing-lobster umbrella."

Her breath hitches slightly. "What are you saying?"

I don't like her being over me in this moment. I let go of her hands, grip her hips, and use my weight to flip us, tangling the sheet in the process.

"We're happening. I think you feel it too. You put in the effort tonight, showing up, getting to know my kid, and hell, you didn't run away. You may have looked like a deer in headlights once or twice, but you stayed."

"I do feel it. It's just…"

"April. But you will tell her next time you see her, or I swear to God that I will do it for us. Do you understand?" There is an edge in my tone that I think surprises her.

She slowly nods. "Okay. You're right, it's time."

"Good." I kiss her brow. "But not tomorrow. Tomorrow, you stay here and wait for me to come home."

Piper reaches her hand up to touch my cheek as she

smiles warmly. "I'm not sure I'm any good at wearing an apron and cooking dinner, but I can pretend."

I growl low because the thought will keep me going tomorrow when I'm yelling at the new recruits on the field.

"I can have a chef come," I offer.

She chortles and rolls her eyes. "I love how you say it like it's nothing. But it's okay, I'll swing by Jolly Joe's for coffee, work on my laptop, and pick something up from the grocery store."

"Sounds good." I lie next to her and let out a long breath. "Sleep. We probably need a few hours of that. I'll try not to wake you when my alarm goes off."

"Don't worry. I'm not going anywhere."

I can't help but taunt her. "You have really developed since that first night." I smirk to myself.

She playfully slaps me then cuddles into my arms. "Funny, old man."

"Ouch. You're getting vicious."

"Nah, just getting comfortable."

And that's exactly how I want her.

———

I RUB my eyes and walk into the kitchen. The house is dark except for the small light next to the coffee machine that is on a timer.

Looking up from straightening my hoodie, I stop in my tracks when I see Piper leaning against the counter in only my shirt with my coffee thermos in hand.

"You really are trying to shock me in the kitchen these days, huh?" I say, and I'm completely adoring her even more. Walking slowly to her, I take the thermos she offers.

"Snuck down here when you were in the shower. Thought I could wish you a good day."

I kiss her good morning and wrap an arm around her middle. "Next time join me in the shower."

"Uh-uh. I think you have a schedule to keep, Coach." She flashes her eyes at me.

"I'll break every damn rule if it's worth it."

Our eyes meet and a brief silence overtakes us.

"I think it might just be."

And I hear it in her floaty voice that her words mean us.

16

PIPER

I look over the design on my tablet and nervously await my grandmother to give me feedback. The other day, I spent the whole afternoon sitting outside Hudson's house, overlooking the lake and drawing away. Creativity just flowed out

"You think April will like it?" I ask as we stand over the table with my tablet.

My grandmother with her small frame looks up at me, her glasses perched on her nose. "It's beautiful. The lines along the back really bring the wow factor." She takes her glasses off and walks to her sofa.

I smile proudly to myself as I close the cover on the tablet. "I'll show her later today. I've been tossing ideas at her for the last few weeks, but now I feel like I can show her the final blueprint, you know?" I say and sit down on the opposite sofa. My cheeks hurt from the smile that doesn't want to fade. Not only for the boho chic design on my tablet but life lately.

"Have some tea, dear. You look like you could use something to calm yourself down." There is amusement in her voice.

Quickly, I whip my eyes in her direction, and I see that she is assessing me with a self-assured smirk.

I tuck a few strands of hair behind my ear. "I'm…"

"There's a man." She waves a finger at me. "I'm disappointed you haven't told me sooner."

The gushing smile spreads, and my heart feels full. "There is, and I haven't told you because, well… I wasn't sure where to begin."

She brings her cup to her lips for a sip before placing it back on her saucer. "You invite him to Friday dinner, that's how you begin. You can make up for all the ones you've missed nearly every week the past month or two. That was the first giveaway that you met someone, and the second…"

"There's a second?" I sit up straight.

"Yes. It's your face and the way you just explained the dress you drew, a dress that I'm not entirely sure was inspired by April."

I shake my head. "What? What are you insinuating?"

"You poured your own emotion into it."

My smile fades, and I have to think about her train of thought. It leads me to internally admit that maybe she's right.

"Tell me everything I need to know."

"Hudson is… different."

She touches her pearl earring. "They always are, dear. Now, will you get more specific or do I need to head onto the socials and stalk you for clues?"

"Socials? You're going to show up on my feed again, aren't you?" I grin to myself because this woman has no qualms about modern technology.

"When it comes to you? Yes. Which way will it be? Give

your dear old grandmother the facts or I log in to my fake account."

I laugh at her antics and lean back on the sofa. "Why am I not surprised? And sorry to disappoint but you won't find anything online. We have been a little off the radar, and besides, I don't really post personal things online."

"Fine. But I'm waiting... Details, please. Does April approve?"

Just like that my elated look fades as guilt hits me. "She doesn't know. Not yet, anyway."

"I'm truly touched that you're sharing the news with me first." My grandmother touches her heart for theatrics.

I sigh and look away then back. "It's a little complicated."

"How so?"

"Hudson is April's uncle. I didn't know who he was until after we'd already met."

"Uncle, hmm, he's older then?"

"Yes."

A warm reassuring smile graces her lips. "Your grandfather was older than me. It's better that way. You need someone who will lead you and support you, who knows what he's doing in both life and the bedroom—"

My palm flies up. "Do *not* finish that sentence. Geez, have we not established boundaries?"

"There is no harm in talking about sex, dear. You design lingerie, for crying out loud. I don't live under a rock. I'm sure you model your collection for him, as you should with those legs."

I haven't blinked in the last thirty seconds as I sit here with a blank face.

"So April doesn't know. You think she will not be pleased?"

"I don't know what to think other than the dynamics make it an awkward situation."

She waves a finger at me with a tsk, and I feel like I'm eight again and stole candy from her jar. "Be bold."

"I'm going to be. Hudson thinks like you, says things are only complicated if I make it that way."

"What does this wise man do?"

"He coaches football."

My grandmother's eyes grow full of interest, and she grabs her phone from the arm of the sofa. I roll my eyes because I know exactly what she's doing.

"Want me to save you the trouble? He coaches the Winds."

Her finger scrolls the screen with vigor. "My goodness, Hudson Arrows is a looker. Certainly has quite a few articles that I shall read later. I've heard about him, I mean who hasn't in this city, right?"

I hold my hand up. "Me. I didn't," I answer blandly.

"I could see you on his arm. He must be good to you if you've cancelled on me more than once lately." She looks up with a contrite smile before resuming her research. "I expect to meet him as soon as possible."

"May be hard, as it's training season and they train up by his lake house on Lake Spark."

Her mouth falls open. "That's where you've been hiding away? It's beautiful there. Your grandfather used to take me there for romantic weekends. Is there still that old inn by the water?"

I nod. "Yes, and there is an old-fashioned candy store. Everyone seems nice up there. A refreshing change from the busy city."

"Sounds like a perfect match then."

"You know, it feels good to share this with someone. At

first, I wasn't sure if we were just... well, anyways, some-thing inside me keeps telling me to take little steps."

My grandmother leans back and taps her fingertips on the sofa. "A good strategy considering your history, but don't let one bad apple make you hesitate for life. Don't be afraid to take risks, Piper."

"I think I'm slowly realizing that."

"Good. Now that I know your secret and plan on finding out every detail about your prince, then you have no reason to come up with ridiculous excuses for not visiting me."

I smile nervously. "The conference on organic fabric in Wichita was a giveaway, huh?"

She pulls at her earring. "I mean, it was creative, dear."

"I just hope April sees all of this as a positive too."

"Go. Go talk to her. Falling in love is better when you can share the news with a friend."

I stand up. "I think so too."

And I'm not sure, but I think both parts of her statement ring true; sharing with a friend and falling in love.

———

APRIL and I wait for the bagels that we ordered from the deli counter.

"I have the final design," I tell her as someone hands me my plate.

"Oh." April doesn't sound enthusiastic. "I hope they didn't toast the bagel, they always do that even when I ask them not to."

Huh, she's diverting the conversation to bagels.

We walk to a table and sit down to inspect our sandwiches.

"It looks not toasted today. You're in luck," I add and know that I can only stall for so long.

"I guess," she replies, slightly deflated.

It seems that now is as good a time as any.

I take a deep breath. "There is something I kind of wanted to talk to you about," I begin.

April looks up from her basket plate and the potato chip she's playing with. "You met someone."

I'm surprised she guessed it; she's making it easy for me. "Yeah. How did you know?"

"You're never around anymore, as you always have some work trip." She shrugs her shoulder. "Is it mystery guy?"

I swallow. "It is. I lied and it wasn't a bust at all. I just wasn't sure where it was going."

"I get it, maybe." April seems unusually calm, somber even.

"I really wanted to tell you, but I needed to wrap my head around it."

She nods slowly in understanding.

"And the thing is, I need to tell you something else." Nerves fill me, seeping through my veins, and I feel like I may throw up, but I need to do this. Hudson and I have become the worst-kept secret since so many people know. I hope April will be understanding and maybe we can even laugh about the coincidence that Hudson is the guy I met.

"Jeff and I ended our engagement last night," April blurts out, and tears pool in her eyes.

Oh, shit.

"What?"

This wasn't what I had planned for today, and concern for April overpowers anything I thought of saying.

I'm quick to slide off my chair and come to sit next to her.

I touch her shoulder as she wipes away a tear. "What happened?"

"I'm just not good enough to be someone's wife," she cries.

"That's not true," I say, quick to assure her. "It's his loss."

She wipes her cheek with the back of her hand. "Oh, come on, Piper, you never really liked Jeff."

I tip my head to the side in doubt of how honest I should be, because yes, I didn't quite see them as forever, but when your friend seems happy then what are you to do? "It doesn't mean that I would want you to feel like this."

"I feel so numb," she wails.

I hug her and rub circles on her back. "It'll get better, I promise."

"Easy for you to say when you're in the lovey-dovey stage with some hot older man."

There's a twist in my gut, knowing that she may hate that she just said that when she discovers the truth. Maybe we should just lay everything on the table now. Yet when I look at April and she appears so sad, I feel like it isn't the right moment. I was so in my element that I didn't press her when we came into the bagel shop, even when I noticed she seemed off.

My friend is in pain, and I don't want to take the chance that I add to her temporary misery. Today is not the right time to tell her who the mystery man really is.

So I hug her and don't say a word.

17

HUDSON

I throw my water bottle to the side in a fit of anger. The assistant coaches around me take a step back as we walk along the field in the late-morning sun.

"I want to see Lewis in my office this afternoon. Is he not following workouts in his own time? He's out of shape and doesn't seem to have studied any plays at all. This isn't the standard I expect."

"I'll set up a meeting," Arnold our team manager pipes up.

"Good. I want him off the field for the rest of practice. He's a distraction and needs a rest." I rub the back of my neck in pure aggravation.

Lewis, my second season linebacker is pissing me off, and unlucky for him it's on the wrong day. Ever since Piper told me the other day about April, I've been conflicted.

I wanted to reach out to April, but from my understanding, only Piper knows, which means April would know Piper and I are in contact. As much as I don't care that April knows that fact, I am sensitive to April's moment of despair. But this means we're stuck in a holding pattern until April finds out.

Yep, unlucky Lewis for pissing me off on the wrong day.

"Kimberly is here," one of the assistant coaches announces.

Ugh, just what I need now, the team's new PR coordinator who focuses on social media. She just graduated from college, and her idea of building buzz is creating little videos every day and posting them online. When she asked if she could take a video of what my lunch was, that was the day I almost lost faith in humanity.

I roll my eyes before I rub my face when I witness her clearly flashing an overly sweet smile at one of my players as she walks my way.

"Hudson!" she calls out with a little wave. "We need to go over the calendar."

"Can't this wait? I want to do one more drill with my guys."

She looks down at her tablet. "The schedule says they should have a break now."

I hear Arnold chuckle under his breath, and I give him side-eye. "You handle the team; I'll get this over with."

He slaps a hand on my shoulder. "Just remember that sponsors love the shit she spews out."

"Don't I know it." I turn my attention to Kimberly, cross my arms, and smile politely. "What's on the agenda today?"

She flings her hair behind her shoulder. "Well, we need to finalize details for the pre-season team dinner, the charity BBQ, and the press conference coming up. I think you have the press conference under control, but I need you to confirm how many guest seats you want for the dinner and BBQ."

"You know I do those things solo."

"I know, but someone from the events team mentioned sometimes a Drew and Lucy come?" She studies her screen, clearly having no idea who they are.

"It's okay, Kimberly, they're my son and daughter-in-law. We don't actively advertise that fact."

She smiles genuinely. "Oh, okay. Well, let me know if they'll be coming. Which brings me to the other question." She attempts to hold in her smile. "Do we need to plan for a plus-one for your upcoming functions? Otherwise... damn it, why do they make me do this," she mutters to herself, and I appreciate that we've established enough trust that she can curse in front of me.

"Spit it out."

"Marketing wants to know if they can agree to a feature on you that may emphasize that you're a bachelor. They think it draws in the female demographic." I can tell she doesn't enjoy being the messenger.

I'm quick to answer. "Plan for a plus-one."

"Really?"

I glance over at the guys setting up for a scrimmage. "Yes."

"So... there is someone?"

My attention turns back to her. "Yes."

"Care to elaborate? Because they will only send me back here tomorrow." Her face is pleading.

"There is someone in my life, so yes, Piper will be with me."

The thing about aggravation is it shoots determination through me and sends me on a direct path to what I want. I know April will figure everything out soon, and that means that Piper and I can continue to take steps, and I want nothing more than to have Piper by my side.

"That is such an adorable name. Can I have a last name, social handles, and any dietary restrictions?" Kimberly returns to business mode.

"Nope. How about we keep it easy."

Kimberly stomps her foot in slight frustration. "You know Smith's wife started posting several times a day about a day in the life of a football wife, often taking pictures and videos when she visits him at practice, videos of what she cooks him for breakfast before training, those kinds of things. She gained a hundred thousand followers in one week. Fans love that stuff."

I hold my hand up. "No disrespect to Smith's wife, but Piper is not that kind of woman." Piper carries herself with a sort of demeanor that my parents would call classy, yet behind closed doors, she's the best kind of dirty.

Kimberly holds up a finger. "One post. One picture when she visits you at training. Give us something."

"Can we focus on my guys again, please? What's happening to that whole football-players-with-puppies charity event? I mean, sign me up for that. It's puppies," I tell her half-heartedly.

"Fine. I get the hint."

"Good. Now I need to get back to coaching." I throw a thumb over my shoulder and walk back to centerfield.

I shake my head. As much as Kimberly's suggestions are ridiculous, I can't help but smile at the idea of everyone knowing who my girl is, making it clear Piper is off-limits and I take complete claim for her. And hot damn, I'm sure we would blow up the marketing department's social media quota.

———

MY SISTER CATHERINE walks into my office at the training facility that is my home for most hours of the day as we prepare for the new season. It's a mess at this moment due to having extra screens up so I can compare plays and footage.

She was in the area to collect intel for one of her depositions and called if she could stop by, and I have an afternoon break that I don't normally take.

But this is perfect timing, as I was going to call her anyway to share the latest news in my life.

"Hey, big sis," I greet her with a hug.

She hugs me back. "Hey, trouble." She sits on a chair in front of my desk while I head in the direction of my small fridge

She admires the new photo from Drew's wedding, a photo of me and the happy couple. "Good photo. He's settling into married life? Or have you not seen him yet since the wedding?"

"I saw him the other week when he delivered a shelf he made."

I bring her a sparkling water then slide my phone off the desk, unlock my screen, and show her the photo of Drew's latest creation.

Catherine examines the screen. "It's beautiful. I wonder if he could make me one."

I admire the woodwork in the photo and smile at the fact that Piper left a creepy lobster statue on top of a book. She said it brings luck, and she had it in her car as she was moving things from her office to storage.

"You know he will."

She taps the screen with her nail. "Send me this photo so I have an idea of the measurements." Catherine makes herself at home and opens her bottle of water. "I won't stay long, just wanted to quickly chat in person," she calls out.

I head behind my desk and let out a sigh of relaxation because it's the first moment of the day that I don't need to discuss football.

"April and Jeff broke off their engagement," she explains.

I ditch my seat and head to my coffee machine on the side table and hit the button for a cup of caffeine that now seems like nirvana since we are heading straight into a serious conversation. "I know."

"How? She only just told me last night."

Grabbing my cup, I have no intention to lie to my sister. "Piper told me."

My sister tilts her head in curiosity as she studies me. "I didn't realize you two had contact."

Sitting down, I lean back, throw my feet on my desk, and take a sip of my coffee. "Want to make this about your daughter or me?" I counter.

"I'm concerned about April. She must be heartbroken, but I hate myself for not giving in to the red flags and telling April she could do better."

"Fate stepped in then." I hold my coffee up to her in a toast. "I'll reach out to April if you want. Maybe she could use a weekend here at Lake Spark."

"That would be a good idea." Catherine brushes a piece of lint off her slacks. A silence overtakes us, and she examines me before giving me a pointed look. "You're sleeping with my daughter's best friend?"

I grin because of her bluntness. "I would like the think we are more than that, but yes. Piper and I met before we realized how we're connected. Funny, huh?" I stay calm and collected, in fact unaffected by my sister's facial expression of intrigue.

"Yet April has no clue," she highlights the fact.

"Piper was going to tell her the other day, but April wasn't in a great place. I'd do it myself, however they should figure it out between them. I don't want to get in the way of their friendship."

"How noble of you." I sense sarcastic undertones in her

words. Catherine gives me a stern look before she throws her hand in the air. "You're right, though, it's for them to work it out." She studies me for another hot second. "Piper? Really? I mean, she is a lovely girl, don't get me wrong. But your niece's best friend? Like, really? Is this a mid-life crisis thing?"

I give her a pointed unimpressed look and swing my feet off my desk to sit up straight. "It's not. She's good for me."

"April may be crushed."

"Why? Wouldn't she want her best friend and favorite uncle together?" I place my coffee to the side.

My sister gives a short laugh. "Listen to that statement you just said. And I don't know, maybe she'll be thrilled. She has a lot going on right now, so I can't predict it."

"Well, I'm not going to hide my relationship with Piper anymore."

"Uh-oh. Bullheaded Hudson is coming out. You were this way when you discovered you have a son. Determined as hell and nobody could get in your way. Just be sensitive, please, it involves my daughter," she reminds me.

I nod in understanding. "Is it so wrong to grab hold of what you want when you discover what you have?"

Catherine chortles. "Well, I'll be damned. You are under a spell, and let's just all hope it doesn't wear off when you're out in the open, no longer sneaking around, or that Piper is just as ready as you seem about a future."

Her statement takes me off guard because she's right. Piper needs to be on the same wavelength, or we have no chance.

"Is that concern I hear?" My brows lift.

She folds her arms over her chest and taps her fingers along her forearms. "It's logic. She's young, maybe doesn't want to jump into all the things you do, well, at least not on your timeline. But heaven help us if you actually listen to me."

I smile to myself because I hear the caring undertones but admire her ability to still lecture me as an adult. "I'll take it into consideration."

My phone in my pocket vibrates, and I pull it out to see that Piper sent a message.

PIPER

> Hey, I know you're supposed to be in focus mode during training, but I'm going to try and head up to Lake Spark later this week. I'll drive up, avoid foxes and killer pinecones. Hopefully won't have terrible timing again too. I want to see you.

A hint of a smile tilts on my lips, and my sister's advice now only hangs by a thread in the back of my head.

Because I've got everything under control. Even the slither of doubt within can't shake my standpoint that I'll get exactly what I want.

18

HUDSON

With my hands in my jean pockets, I lean against the door pane to stare at the woman in my bed. It's the kind of view a guy could get used to. Piper is wearing one of my old hoodies, legs bare, and her knees are up which means the glimpse of bare skin confirms she only has a thong on.

She tosses her tablet to the side as she looks up to greet me with warm eyes and a welcoming smile. "There you are."

"Making yourself at home?" I smirk and head into my bedroom while I take off my t-shirt and jeans. My body is drained, but I have a woman who is beckoning me to fall into her arms between the sheets.

Piper doesn't move, instead lying there waiting, watching, and looking confident that she is supposed to be the queen of my bed, and pats the spot next to her to invite me to join her. "I knew you would be late, and I just wanted a cozy night to catch up on emails."

I set my knee on the bed and crawl to her to steal a kiss. "I was waiting for this." I speak against her lips before the tips of our tongues touch for a little tease.

Her hands come up to frame my face. "You seem tired."

A short laugh escapes me. "I've been up since five and it's now almost eleven. This is usual as we prepare for pre-season games."

"You drove?"

"I have a driver for the next few weeks. There is no way I'm driving this late after a long day, plus I can use the drive to go over notes for tomorrow's training."

"Come to bed. I'll massage your shoulders." Her thumb swirls on my cheek.

I would love to collapse on the mattress, but I'm a man who survived a day of sun, running up and down a field, and standing around with sweaty guys needing a lecture. I give her a peck on the lips real quick. "A two-minute shower then I'm back."

Piper pretends to pout and grabs my arm as I leave. "I can be of assistance."

"Oh, I know you can, but I'll be fast," I promise.

She nods in agreement.

The moment, I get the shower on, dim the lights, and throw some music on the Bluetooth, I'm regretting not dragging Piper in here. But I need a few minutes to myself after this day, and even the drive back wasn't peaceful, as one of my assistant coaches had sent a long email that I needed to process.

My evening shower is a sort of ritual to turn off my football brain and refocus on other aspects of my life.

Warm water cascades down my body as soon as I step in. A deep breath and I can already feel the thoughts float into my head about the fact that Piper is here and finding a routine at my house with ease. But a few hours every night are not enough. I'm asking a lot that she always comes here to Lake Spark, but I get the impression she prefers it here to the city anyhow. Then again, once the season starts, then my time here will also be minimal.

Turning the water off, I grab a towel, and two minutes later I'm back to my bed. Piper is now only in my t-shirt. In fact, I think she has been wearing my clothes at night more than her own line of pajamas that she designed.

Piper pulls open the duvet to offer me a spot while I grab a pair of boxer briefs, never breaking our gaze.

"Kept the bed warm," she proudly states.

It's only a second after my ass hits the mattress that Piper is on top of me, straddling me, with her hands resting on my shoulders as I sit against the headboard. Despite her warm heat on top of my dick, she isn't even being sexual. She's caring.

Her fingers begin to knead into my shoulders. "Is it always like this? You're a little tense."

"This is normal. It's long days now, and when games start, it's a little less long but more pressure. Welcome to my life for the next six months." I rub my hands along her fore-arms and take in how good it feels to have someone massaging me with purpose.

"I have to say that it sounds awful, but you seem to enjoy your job. It's just… maybe I'm beginning to really under-stand why you haven't had time for… other things." She's acting sheepish, but I know what she means.

I stop her from massaging me further and have to smirk at her thought. "As in a relationship?"

A knowing grin is faint on her lips. "Maybe that is what I was getting at."

I comb my fingers through her hair because her lush brown locks frame her face and it's slightly distracting, as I just want to wrap her hair around my hand and pull her mouth to mine. "Partly, yes. But if you put in the effort then it can work. I never wanted to put in the effort... until now."

Piper shimmies closer to my body, causing my cock to twitch, but I stay on point and pull her closer to me to wrap her tightly in my arms.

"Summer training is over in a week," she says, "then it's pre-season games and then game season where you stay in a hotel the night before home games too." She's showing off her knowledge that is a mix of what I've told her and exploring the internet.

"I hate that time isn't on our side, we only have small windows. Speaking of which, stop by the stadium tomorrow for lunch," I suggest.

Her face freezes for a brief second. "Oh, I kind of planned to do my usual coffee in town, walk around, and some old lady mentioned they have a drawing class by the gazebo every day during the summer."

My eyes raise to her, and I'm kind of taken aback that she's pushing back. "Piper."

"Hudson," she returns my authoritarian tone.

"I don't like this avoidance. I've been patient, but now is the time to rip the band-aid off and tell April. Besides, I want to see you more outside of our bubble. Soon, I won't be at Lake Spark as much."

Her lips quirk out, and she seems sad by that thought. "I'll miss it here."

"Using me for my house," I joke.

She playfully pushes my shoulder. "I like it here. The home you built, the man who lives here. When I'm here with you, it's our own little world."

"We get to have the whole world as ours if you speed up the avoidance of truth with my niece issue. And my house is your house, so use it even if I'm away."

Her eyes turn appreciative. "Thank you, and I hear what you're saying about April. I just wanted to give her time, nor did I want to flaunt my romantic life to her when her own combusted."

Another reason that I can't seem to be angry, only annoyed. Piper has a heart of gold and doesn't want to hurt her best friend. But in the process, I'm drowning in limbo and it's no fun.

"Soon, Piper," I nearly chide.

"I hear you. I promise."

"Good, because I told the team publicist to expect you at some of our events and games," I inform her confidently.

"W-what?" she nearly shrieks.

A cocky smirk tilts on the corner of my mouth. "You heard me."

Her face lightens gently, and she glances at her fingers drawing circles against my chest. "It's a big deal, Hudson. It puts me in the public eye, and I'm not used to that." There's more to it, I hear it in her voice, but I don't press.

"I respect that, but that is kind of what you sign up for when you're with me." I lean down to kiss her fingers.

"You keep your son out of the press," she is quick to remind me.

"True. But it's easier. The press is a little too eager to know my romantic life. Hell, if I have to stand through another photo shoot for a bachelor coach article then I may have to punish you for that," I say in an attempt to lighten the mood.

Piper rolls her eyes. "How about we save this talk for tomorrow when we're not as tired?"

I study her for a second, and she has a valid point because my eyes desperately want to close. "Sure."

"You can slide into me whenever you want," she offers with a mischievous sly grin.

We both begin to shuffle around to get comfortable for the night. "That is some offer. You know I may just take you up on it at 4:55 in the morning before my alarm goes off."

"Sounds like a perfect way to wake up."

We both lie on our sides and face one another, her leg hooking over my hip and our hands resting on one another.

"Everything is perfect when I'm with you," I faintly whisper.

Her lips twitch which informs me that the statement affected her. "Can't argue with that."

For tonight, that's enough.

———

WALKING OUT ONTO THE FIELD, I notice the group congregating near the twenty-yard line, a mix of football players in practice uniforms and women all cooing in a circle. I glance up at the stands, as we now have open practices which means fans can watch, and in this very moment, they're all standing and taking photos.

"What in the world is going on?" I ask Arnold who is by my side. It was lunch break for an hour, but we just ate in my office to discuss the team.

Arnold smiles and tips his head in the direction of the group. "Jefferson's wife had a baby the other week, remember? Even scheduled the induction on our day off." My eyes go wide, as that is some commitment, although not the first time that I heard of a player's wife doing that if the stork decides to deliver a baby during season. "His wife must have brought the baby to visit."

That explains why everyone seems to be in a good mood.

Often, players have their partners or family watching practice or stopping by. Jesus, Smith's wife drives me crazy when she stops by without fail to kiss her husband, take a selfie, and post it online. Mostly because I seriously doubt her intentions of real love and wonder if she is more interested in the fame.

But truthfully, I know there is a twinge of jealousy inside of me that a twenty-four-year-old linebacker gets something that I don't—a romantic relationship. I glance toward the parking lot, and disappointment flickers inside my stomach because Piper didn't stop by. In reality, it's probably for the best because it was a tight window of time and I needed to work anyhow. But even a kiss would have given me a little extra energy and pep.

Arnold and I walk toward the group. I hear someone call out *Coach Arrows is here*. For some reason my name causes everyone to step back to create a path and grow quiet, as if I'm the boogeyman. My path lands me in the middle of the circle with everyone's eyes on me, or at least I feel them, but I'm staring only at one player in uniform and light pads holding a tiny squishy baby.

Jefferson looks up at me nervously. "Oh hey, Coach."

I smile with ease and hope it reassures him that I'm not the devil. "Your son?"

"Yeah. Getting him into the game early."

I turn my attention to his side, to his wife who's wearing one of those carrier things. "Congratulations."

The petite blonde woman who looks slightly tired smiles. "Thank you. We'll get out of everyone's hair now."

I look down at my watch and see that we should be starting, as we have a strict schedule and a long afternoon ahead of us, but I can't bring myself to be a hard-ass. "It's okay, we'll start in five minutes."

Jefferson's smile grows wide.

Leaving everyone to it, I head away from the group to the table on the sidelines. That short walk is enough time for me to question my soft demeanor that just happened. I normally reserve it for my private life. I'm changing, probably because I feel like these same moments that my players, my son, hell, most of the world get are now within my reach.

Doesn't mean I will go easy on them during practice, though. I'm going to make these guys work damn hard, with a completely selfish motive to let us off a little early tonight so I can finish my discussion with Piper.

———

PIPER LOOKS up from the glass of water she just poured from the fridge dispenser. I'm home early, although I will need to watch footage of the practice later in my office. I texted Piper when I was in the car.

"Want me to attempt to cook? I started to make snacks." She walks to me, oblivious that I'm agitated. It's only when she attempts to kiss me and I don't put in the effort to kiss back that she senses my mood. "Everything okay?"

I shake my head gently as our eyes meet in a tense stare. "No. We need to talk."

She tips her head back, with her smile now faltering, but keeps her arms looped around my neck. "What's wrong?"

"I'm done waiting. I need to know that you're ready to move forward, no more stalling. I know you want to, but I can't figure out why exactly you're hesitating." I unhook her arms from around my neck and hold her wrists gently up to keep her in my hold.

"What do you mean?"

I snicker. "I'm done running around like we're a secret. If you can't make the jump, then what are we doing?"

"Hudson," she sighs.

"Don't do that. Don't come up with excuses. We both know that what we have is more than what either of us thought would happen the night we met." I yank her closer, drop her wrists, then weave my hands into her hair. There is passion in my movement, and Piper draws in a breath as a response. "I'm not going to wait; my patience is wearing thin. I want you by my side no matter where we are. You're driving me crazy, you're always on my mind, and when you're here, I just want more and more. I think I've warned you that I'm a man who jumps right in, but I only jump in when it's right."

Her eyes are almost pleading. "I'm going to tell April, okay."

"Great. But there's more for us, I need more commitment. I want you cheering for me on the sidelines, visiting me on breaks so I can fuck you in my office or car. Let me meet your grandmother and tell me what you see in our future when you're lying in my arms." I hear the vulnerability in my voice.

I continue my explanation of what's going on in my head. "You feel it inside of yourself that you want us, but you can't say the words that you're all in." I walk her backward until her back hits the edge of the wall. I let her wrists go and kiss her hard until she murmurs while she fists the fabric of my shirt at my chest. I kiss the corner of her mouth then speak against her lips. "I'm going to give you an ultimatum, but I don't believe I need to. You know how I know you want us?"

"Enlighten me," she rasps with her eyes drawing a line up and down my body.

I step between her knees to part her legs open while our foreheads touch, and I sneak my fingers up her thighs and under her skirt. "You let me come inside of you and I know you're not on birth control." My fingers dive into her panties to touch her soft heat, already wet. Her face looks panicked as if she has been caught out. "I'm not mad, baby, I could have stopped us, and I didn't." I don't break our connection and the tips of our noses touch.

"I haven't done it intentionally, I just… I can't explain it. Sorry, I should be more care-"

"Shh." I kiss her lips and continue to stroke her pussy. "Your body already knows what you want before your thoughts catch up. It takes two, and I'm a selfish man who wants to fill you up, and I don't care if you get pregnant, so I'm not going to say *we* should be careful. Hell, I'm not getting any younger, and the thought of you pregnant with my child is something I envision. But the point is that you wouldn't take the risk unless you have the trust and felt it was worth it. Tell me I'm wrong."

Piper frantically shakes her head as her fingers fumble with my jeans. "I can't. You're right. I trust whatever is happening between us." Her head falls forward and rests against my shoulder.

"It's our future, that's what is happening." I guide her arms over her head against the wall.

"You want to know what makes me hesitate, what scares me?" I hear so much vulnerability in her voice.

I press my forehead against hers. "Tell me," I whisper. My eyes lock with hers to encourage her to speak.

"We're moving fast, but if I blink, I know I could have it all with you because I see it. I've never experienced this before."

Her answer is exactly what I needed to hear.

We press our bodies against one another, and we kiss, hungry, before I drop to my knees and bring her foot to my shoulder, giving me ample opportunity to travel up her smooth thigh with my mouth, brushing my lips delicately before inhaling her scent and licking over the fabric of her drenched panties.

I feel her losing her balance, and her hands land on my head to brace herself. "What are you doing to me?"

A devilish chuckle escapes my throat. "Making you mine."

"I'm already yours." She breathes out as her hips curve in my direction.

I needed to hear that, which causes me to change our course. Standing, I hoist her up onto the counter beside us, and immediately I hook my arms under her knees to splay her out. Our mouths fuse together, and I feel the urgency to take her. I bend down and dive between her legs, yank her panties to the side, and get a taste.

"You're soaking, Piper," I mutter as I keep busy.

"And you're eager," she counters. Her breath is thick with an equal desire to get lost in one another.

"For us? You have no idea." My tongue lashes out against her pussy.

Her hands wind into my hair. "Hudson," she cries out.

I run my mouth back up to her lips and cover her mouth with my own. I feel like a man possessed. A man who wants to be consumed by her.

She begins to drag her shirt up and off, and of course, I assist her. When her shirt goes flying in the air, I'm already tugging her bra cup down her breast and suckling on her nipple. Her head falls back, and a soft moan escapes her lips. I move to her other little bud and twirl my tongue and nip her skin.

"Ah, so good," she hums.

I pull back slightly, with her legs still hooked around my arms. "Good," I chuckle under my breath. "It only gets better from here, baby."

I unzip my jeans and pull them down just enough. In a rapid movement, I slide her to the edge of the counter. Tonight, I'm lacking a bit of finesse, but we have confirmations to make.

My mouth trails up her neck, causing her to lie back on the counter. I drag her arms up over her head and pin them down. Her entire body arches up against me, a sort of surrender. Our kisses are messy, and her breath is heavy.

"I want all of you. Don't you realize you're mine? Your pussy will only ever feel my cock from this moment forward. So when you go to sleep tonight in my bed, next to me where you belong, lying against my chest, remember what you choose, because I want all in."

I don't wait for her to answer. I plunge into her, and we both moan at the sudden movement. Her hands walk her upper body up to sitting, one arm encircling around my neck. I can feel her breath against my skin.

"I understand," she gasps.

I continue to pump in and out of her without an ounce of grace. Reaching between us, I grab the edge of my shirt, and she helps me pull it up over my head, and soon it lands on the floor. Our bodies are inseparable, our hands glued to one another, wandering and exploring. But every kiss feels more intense. The emotional element is underlying which only makes our senses work in overload.

Every time Piper breathes my name, it only encourages me to fuck her a little harder. She isn't complaining either, because her legs wrap tighter around my waist with our bodies moving together in a rhythm.

A sheen of sweat breaks out on my skin and her hair is a mess. She looks like a woman at my mercy, but the fact she clenches around my length reminds me she's an equal partner in our journey to bring each other to the edge.

Piper tightens her arms around me and buries her head into the crook of my neck before kissing the base of my throat.

I pause in movement but remain inside of her as I cradle her head in my hands. "Do you understand?"

"Yes."

I kiss her eyelids that hood closed. "I'm crazy about you." I kiss her jawline. "It isn't just infatuation; the damn future is with you because I'm in love with you."

Her eyes shoot open, and her body is near panting, but the corners of her mouth twist into a subtle smile. "I was sensing that, but I like hearing it." Ah, she's being a smartass. "I'm in love with you too, and I'm not just saying that because your hard cock is inside of me."

I laugh because that's Piper, surprising me with her mouth at random moments. Our lips seal together as I move again, this time a bit more frantic.

Finally, when she's trembling in my arms, I'm chasing right behind her with a few more thrusts, and then I'm doing exactly what I plan on doing every chance I get, filling her up because she is mine.

19

PIPER

"Can't keep up, old man?" I holler over my shoulder to Hudson as we walk up the path in the woods behind Hudson's house.

He quickly runs to catch up and grabs me by the waist, pulling me against his body causing me to squeal. "Watch it there or I may need to teach you a lesson." Playfully, he swats my ass.

It's Sunday which means he kind of has a day off. Or at least the morning off; Hudson and his coaching staff are meeting later at Catch 22 to discuss the team. We decided to do an early-morning walk to get some fresh air.

I look up to meet his lips for a kiss.

"I was admiring the view, you should too."

"I guess I get into my power-walking a little too much."

He pulls back and laughs. "I know. It's like take off the heels and throw on some sneakers and you're a bionic bunny."

I stretch my arms into the air. "It's a beautiful day, fresh air, and I'm wide awake."

"You're obviously not sore enough from last night, I'm

not doing my job right." He says that without breaking, but I can only grin.

We begin to walk again, hand in hand. "You also seem very happy." His voice turns sincere.

"I think you know why," I remind him and give him a sly look.

He brings his arm around my shoulders. "Oh, I do. I think we went over it several times last night in bed."

We approach a lookout point at the edge of the tree line that overlooks Lake Spark just as a man in his fifties walks away, with his golden retriever on a leash, and we greet them in passing.

This is such a great view. It's different to Hudson's backyard because we're higher up and looking down. I can see the town square on one side, someone fishing in the middle of the lake, and I spot someone swimming.

"Pete's at it again. No rest for the wicked and old," Hudson comments.

"He has to burn off all those jellybeans."

"He's a good guy. We have a team fundraiser for this children's charity, and he donated like half his candy store. Speaking of which, want to come to practice this week? I mean, I am assuming you can just stay here for a while since you seem to work from my house."

"True. I can work from anywhere, although my grandmother does like to see me in physical form to make sure I'm still alive. But I haven't really thought about the next week, I only packed for a few days."

He chortles a sinister laugh and releases his arm to lean against the railing of the lookout and face me. "Not a factor. You already left a few things last time you were here, you know where the laundry room is, my shirts look good on you, and my favorite solution is how you can just walk around my house naked."

I loll my head to the side slightly with a closed smile. "Valid points, Coach Arrows."

"You're stalling again." Lines form between his brows. "Speak to me."

I roll my lips into my mouth. This man can see through me. "It's…"

He steps into me and is quick to bring his hand to my cheek affectionately. "Go on."

"I'm mentally preparing for people's opinions of me personally." That was a lot easier to admit than I thought.

Hudson nods once, with his eyes filled with understanding before placing a gentle kiss against my temple. "I kind of assumed it had something to do with that."

I rub my cheek into his hand. "It's silly. I'm an adult woman, and I'm not ashamed of anything. I just stay away from public stuff; it's why I never model my lingerie and have someone else handle the marketing stuff. Piper Ginger isn't really me, you know? But Piper Dapper? Well, she didn't enjoy the last round of people's opinions or critique. They made me feel like I was a horrible person."

"Baby, you are not. Anything but. You put others before yourself, and so what, you put yourself first this time. You're allowed to and thank goodness you did."

I shrug. "I keep telling myself that. And I know you do your best to keep a low profile, and I said I didn't care who you are, but I know that you are, well… popular. It will be hard to keep a low profile. Besides, geez, have you seen Smith's wife? If that's the standard I need to follow, then I'm not sure my photos of avocado toast and coffee will suffice." There is a little humor in my tone because I don't want to drag this morning down.

He rolls his eyes. "First off, you don't need to be her. Instead, you are a beautiful woman who has a successful business and knows the meaning of making people happy. All I can say is that I will promise to do my best to protect you."

"I believe you."

"One step, okay? Just come to a practice."

I swallow because a sexy smile wants to form on my mouth. "I *may* be intrigued to see you in action."

"I bet you are. Now, want to power-walk it back to the house, hop in the car, and grab some brunch in town?"

My head perks up. "You mean coffee and cinnamon rolls? I could never say no. I heard a rumor the other day at the general store that they changed the recipe for the cinnamon filling and the knitting club decided to write a letter demanding the old recipe comes back."

"Eavesdropping next to the butcher's counter again?" He flashes me a humorous look.

I scoff a sound. "You know it."

We begin to walk back, but I'm quick to grab his wrist. "Hey… I love you."

His suave grin appears. "Love you too. Now let's go get caffeinated."

I yank his arm again. "Maybe we can take a photo of our coffees next to one another to make it official and send it to your publicist for kicks. You're right, I'm ready to go all in."

An almost vulnerable look appears in his eyes as the corner of his mouth curves up. "I don't know what I love more. The fact that you love me or the fact that you make every conversation enjoyable."

"You get both, Coach Arrows."

He growls and tugs me along. "Fuck me, when you say my name like that I'm a goner."

IT'S A THIRTY-MINUTE WALK BACK, and as we emerge from the tree line, we stop still at the end of the driveway.

My heart nearly skips a beat because April is leaning against her car with her arms crossed.

"Fucking knew it," she grits out, and she doesn't seem impressed.

I glance to my side at Hudson who has an awkward wry smile on.

"April," I say. I had planned on telling her when I was back in the city, but I guess she beat me to it.

"Morning, April, how did you get in?" Hudson asks completely in a normal tone and scratches the back of his neck.

"Your asshole neighbor, the baseball player, sped out of the gate nearly running into me, not even caring, so I drove right in while the gate was open," she explains, with her eyes never leaving me as she has an intense stare.

"Right." Hudson accentuates the T.

There is silence for a beat until April begins to shake her head.

"Funny thing. My mom was showing me a photo of a shelf that Drew made for my uncle, then I noticed the unique statue on it. A lobster. I thought, 'wow, that seems oddly like the one I gave Piper.' Then I remembered that Piper is seeing an older guy." April holds a finger up into the air. "Lucky guess."

I step forward. "I tried telling you last time, but it didn't seem like the right moment."

"It's no big deal," Hudson says. "Now you know, and we can all go for brunch." Hudson is still far too relaxed. "Great." He claps his hands together.

April looks at him like he's crazy. "Fuck that. I need to erase a hell of a lot of information that Piper shared with me about you that is just plain... traumatizing."

My face squinches together. "I swear, I had no idea who he was the night I met him."

"But you both figured it out the night of my enga— that stupid party." I can tell her engagement is understandably a sensitive matter.

Hudson and I glance at one another, then back to April.

I breathe out because I want to be honest. "Yes."

April throws her hands up in the air. "So you have just been coming here to be with my uncle and play housewife? Unbelievable."

I rub the back of my neck. "We had to figure out what we were doing."

"And did you?" She gives me a pointed look.

"I think so."

Hudson pipes up. "You know, I think you two need a moment. I'll be inside. April, don't be mad. Even if you are, unlucky for you, I'm your uncle, so I'm sticking around. As for Piper, she's part of my life now."

"Touching." April isn't amused.

Hudson just shakes his head and walks away, grazing my arm in reassurance as he passes.

I step closer in April's direction. "I promise, I was going to tell you next time I saw you."

"Don't blame this on the current state of my mess of a life. You are my friend, we are supposed to say anything."

"Without judgment?" I wonder and fold my arms over my chest.

She scoffs a laugh. "That's not fair. You're sleeping with my uncle who is old enough to be your father. The rules get a little blurred."

I stand tall. "I know. I've been trying to figure them out."

"Oh my God, Piper. Like, despite my relation to him, how do you live in a city so focused on sports and not know the guy you bang is like sports royalty?"

My hands land on my hips. "I don't follow sports," I justify, and my voice squeaks.

"So, what now? You two are like really *together* together? This isn't some weird passionate tryst?"

"No, it's not. It's the real thing," I confirm.

April pauses in thought for a second, her thoughts clearly in turmoil. She says nothing but returns to the driver's-side door.

"Where are you going?"

She opens the door and looks at me with a sharp stare. "I came to solve the mystery, and I did."

"Okay. Then stay and let's have brunch together. Can't you be happy for us?"

April laughs bitterly. "The thing is, when I think about it, the problem isn't you and my Uncle Bay. I want him happy, and I want you happy. Maybe I even can see you two together. But what *is* the problem is that you both lied to me, for months. It also seems like everyone knew but me. That feels like a betrayal. And right now, when life kind of sucks, it's like a knife. So, congratulations, it's your ability to keep a secret and lie to me that has me questioning our friendship, and until I figure that out, I don't want to speak to you."

"April…" My heart hurts, and I want to stop her, but she is quick to get into her car and turn the engine on.

I throw my arms up in the air because there is nothing I can do now. With remorse, I head back into the house to the living room where I find Hudson pulling on a fresh t-shirt. He must pick up on my look because his neutral expression turns to a frown.

"Where's April?"

"She left. She's angry that I never told her."

Hudson walks to me and rubs my arm for comfort. "April will settle down, you'll see."

"It isn't great. I feel really bad now."

He points a finger at me. "Don't." He's firm. "Give it time. Least she knows now, the hard part is over. We can go public without having to worry if she's aware or not."

"Maybe we should wait on that."

An aggravated breath escapes his mouth. "I'm not going to go in a circle. Piper, I'm losing a little patience. I love that you care about my niece, but I'm in the picture now and need the same thought."

It hits me in that moment. I watched my friend leave, and now I'm staring at the man who I think I've been waiting my whole life for. I may be losing a friend, but I've gained a man who loves me, and I don't want to lose him too.

20

HUDSON

My arms stay firmly folded over my chest, and I know that my serious coach look is plastered across my face. But it's almost time for a mini-break, and it's the third time we have run this play, and in this moment, I'm calling bullshit on the third-time's-the-charm theory.

"In the lines," I call out, reminding my guys to focus instead of ending up a jumbled mess.

"We're getting near the end of training camp; they're a little exhausted, I guess," Arnold pipes up.

I give him a stern look. "All the more reason they need to get it together, as we have a pre-season game next week."

He gives me a look that informs me I should probably calm down.

I grumble loudly and roll my eyes. "Blow the whistle. Break time." My tone is sharp, and I point my finger at him to make my stance clear. "Doesn't mean I'm going to go easy in the afternoon practice. I want to speak to the offense coordinators tonight, and I want to add more names that will be off the roster."

He throws his hands up. "I know, I know."

While he blows the whistle, I look at my tablet to go over the morning's playbook and the list of players that I will soon need to cut. This season it seems to be the rookies that have it more together, or who are at least more focused.

I don't take much notice of the guys grabbing water and walking to the bleachers. This is normally when they quickly catch up with their respective others and confirm their lunch plans. It's only when I hear two of my players mentioning the fresh blood on the sidelines with a whistle that I look up.

I'm ready to swipe those smirks off their faces because I don't need them distracted, and someone has these two mid-twenty-year-olds looking all googly eyed. My head turns to get a glimpse of who has their attention.

The moment my eyes land on Piper in a pink summer dress, high-heeled strappy wedges, and sunglasses on her head, I'm torn inside. I'm completely elated that she's here because I've invited her more times than I can count. But the other half of me feels feral, and I'm quick to head in her direction.

"You both may want to study those drills some more," I mention to the boys in passing, taking slight pleasure in the fact that my role can make their life miserable if needed.

My grin spreads as Piper leans over the railing from the seats with a soft smile, as if she isn't quite sure how she should behave.

"Hi." She nibbles her bottom lip.

"You've finally come… here. I mean, we know you come often."

Her mouth drops open. "Hudson, anyone can you hear you say that." She looks around to check that we're in the clear.

I chuckle as I hop on the step and lean up and over the

railing to kiss her. My hand touches her upper arm, and to the bystanders, I'm giving a respectable kiss, but if only they knew my tongue inside her mouth is giving Piper a preview of later when I plan on re-enacting some dirty-as-fuck positions.

Pulling away gently, my eyes connect with her own and they sparkle in a way.

Piper attempts to give me a smile, but it's weak. For the most part, I know she's happy. We laugh and have good evenings together, but I know my niece giving her the silent treatment weighs on Piper's mind. Still, she made the effort to come and see me at practice, which I know is out of her comfort zone.

"I had to check you're still alive after this morning's smoothie attempt. I just thought that if I added apple this time and nixed the cabbage." She shrugs her shoulder.

A stunted laugh escapes me because yesterday she attempted to make me a green protein shake, and it was a little brutal on the tastebuds. This morning she changed the recipe, and the apple did fuck all.

"It tasted fine," I lie. "Thank you for waking up early this morning, every morning really."

I want that every day until the day I die. This woman in my kitchen with the lights dimmed, five in the morning, and her eagerness to see me off so I have a good day.

"Hazards of dating a hot coach, his schedule kind of sucks." She smirks at me, and her fingers play with the neckline of my t-shirt. "And I kind of owe him since I kept him up past his bedtime."

Have mercy on me, because I love her sultry voice and would do anything to stop the clock and take her right now on the goddamn bench on the sidelines.

She must notice that my mind is thinking impure

thoughts. Piper playfully nudges my other arm with her fist. "It's okay that I'm here, right? I'm not a distraction?" Piper seems to wonder if she is approaching her attempt to surprise me all wrong.

It draws my attention back.

I offer my hand so she can climb over the railing. "Of course, you can be here. Besides, you are the right kind of distraction," I admit.

She lands in front of me, and we look directly into one another's eyes.

"Okay. I mean, I guess the cheerleading outfit can stay in the closet." Now she is testing me, and I throw an arm around her shoulders to walk with her side by side.

"You'll be here for a quick lunch? Or did I bore you already? How long have you been here?" I wonder.

"Maybe twenty minutes, and yes, I will keep watching until lunchtime, but then I'm heading back to the city."

I sigh at the thought, as I hate that she isn't a permanent feature at my home. I make a mental note that we need to streamline our timeline. I haven't discussed it with her, but I don't see why living together can't be an item on our agenda. "I guess I'll see you at a game soon?"

"I'll do my best. My mind is kind of occupied as I need to go back to see my grandmother and hopefully try again with April, or at least see if she will speak to me." I hear her disappointment.

"She'll come around."

Piper doesn't answer, instead surveying the area. "I guess we have an audience."

I tip my head to the side. "We are very much in public. But don't worry about it, only people on the list are here, and the wives of players in a way follow a code, which is keep other people's lives private." I scan the area and indeed we have a few eyes on us.

She leans in and speaks low. "Coach Arrows is kind of hot. He seems demanding and bossy, wouldn't want to get in his bad books." Piper's attempt to hide her giggle falls short. I give her raised brows, as I'm not sure where she is leading her thoughts. She is quick to clarify. "You're more serious when you're on the field. The opposite of laid-back Hudson in ridiculous aprons."

"It's been a rough day. I would like to think I'm more approachable to the guys, but today is brutal, they're tiring quickly."

Piper nods in understanding. Our gaze with one another is, however, broken when Kimberly waves and walks to us.

"Hey, Coach!" She widely smiles, clearly thrilled that I'm not alone.

I give her a short wave. "Hi there." I notice Kimberly keeps her eyes set on Piper. "This is Piper who I mentioned. Piper, this is Kimberly who works on the events-and-marketing team."

"Oh." I hear a lack of enthusiasm, but Piper is a sport and offers a genuine smile. "Nice to meet you."

Kimberly looks between us. "Wonderful to see you here, Piper. We were all a little bummed that we had to cancel the bachelor article on Hudson, then celebrated that Hudson under the love spell would also be a great spin. Someone finally tying him down, you know?" She rambles as she normally does around me.

"Whoa. I'm here. Filter it, Kimberly."

Kimberly shakes her head. "Oh shit. I said that all out loud, didn't I?"

Piper's face doesn't flinch as she waits to see where this conversation is going.

It takes a beat. "…But if you two are going social media official, could you maybe add a Chicago Winds theme somewhere in the photo?"

"For sure. We will absolutely take a photo of two Winds mugs with a comment that breakfast is better together." Piper is completely sarcastic which makes me chortle under my breath.

"That would be wonderful." Kimberly continues without picking up Piper's undertone.

"Oh, I was joking." Piper now looks amused.

Kimberly doesn't stop as she looks at her tablet. "Wait… you're the owner of Piper Ginger?" Piper nods proudly. "I love your stuff. Those pajama bottoms with moon prints are my favorite. I could live in those."

"Thank you. Those are my bestsellers."

"Anything else?" I ask. "I kind of need to get back to what I'm paid for." I do my best to swerve Kimberly away.

Her sight lands on me. "I've sent you an updated schedule for the coming weeks. You have a few morning news slots coming up after you announce the season roster."

"Usual business then. Can we catch up later?" I suggest.

"Sure. Maybe I can go over a few things with Piper and the team engagements coordinator during the next hour of practice?"

I look at Piper who seems lost. "It's just protocol. The dos and don'ts of what can be discussed. Not a big deal since you didn't even know who I was when we met."

"What?!" Kimberly looks at Piper.

She shrugs her shoulders. "I know zero about sports."

"Well, that will change soon."

I grin again. "You okay?" I check with Piper.

"Sure, no problem." Piper seems at ease.

"Great. I will give you two a minute then." Kimberly walks off.

Piper looks at me, clearly entertained. "Have I just walked into a cult and this is my initiation?"

I rub both of her shoulders and hold her gaze. "Nah. It's just a different world, a little closed-off sometimes. People kind of keep their distance unless you're married or engaged to a player."

"Oh." Her eyes flutter.

A smirk spreads on my lips. "We can make that happen if you want."

She scoffs a laugh. "Hudson Arrows, always on the fast track."

"I'm not sure slow is for us." I'm serious, and by the way her face stills for a second, I think she understands my sentiment.

"You haven't even met my grandmother yet." It sounds like a challenge.

"I'll rectify that."

Piper glances away then back at me. "I don't doubt that."

"Don't worry, you're the coach's girl, so by association they may be a little scared of you."

"Duly noted."

I glance at my watch and know that I've already let break carry on for a minute longer, and it may have people thinking I'm going soft.

"I'm happy you're here. Also, that you're not running for the hills after the last five minutes."

She steps closer to me, her hands sliding up my arms to land on my shoulders. "Nah, running for the hills would mean that you would only chase after me, and I like when you lead the way."

There is something about her words that lingers inside me

the rest of the day. Piper seemed at ease after chatting with the team coordinators, and a quick lunch was a refreshing change to my schedule. When I bid her goodbye, I could tell she was at peace yet still missing a piece of her life to make her feel fully calm.

And I have every intention to rectify that.

21

HUDSON

I give my best grin, with my swagger out in full force, as I sit on the sofa across from Piper's grandmother who is examining the gift I brought her, completely welcoming the fact that I showed up unannounced and without Piper's knowledge.

"Don't worry, I made sure it was top quality," I assure her as she sets the bottle of vodka, ideal for martinis, to the side. Adjusting my suit jacket, I didn't put it on for her, but I know this outfit gives me an extra edge.

"You get points for the initiative. My granddaughter has no idea you're here, and I think I like that. Although she will be here soon." The woman's red polished nails tap the sofa arm.

"Well, my schedule is a bit tight these days, and I'm in the city, as our season is about to start. I had an hour to spare and figured that I should cross some essential meetings off my list," I explain and insinuate meeting her.

She understands and a smirk spreads on her face. "My granddaughter talks about you, and don't take it personal that she hasn't dragged you to meet me. I can be... opinionated."

"You have good judgment."

A sound escapes her as she stands and walks to a tray of crystal glasses and alcohol choices in well-designed bottles that hold expensive alcohol along the side of the living room. She goes straight for a scotch, stopping mid-pour to look at me and question with her eyes.

"I never let a good-looking woman drink alone and my driver is downstairs."

I may be laying it on thick, but I can tell she likes to play along, and a minute later when she hands me a glass of amber-colored liquid, she pauses to study me once more before returning to her seat.

This place screams old money or at least decorative tastes that take you back to another era.

"So, what really brings you here, Hudson Arrows?" she asks before taking a sip.

I lean back, confident. "Truthfully, I'm being a selfish man. I'm crazy about your granddaughter, and I figured that I would throw in some tradition. It might make Piper blush like a rose, but I'm used to that."

Ruth snorts a laugh. "I'm sure you keep her satisfied."

My eyes bug out slightly, as this lady's humor is on par with my own. "If I wait for Piper to invite me, then I may be waiting a while, and I know you're important to her."

"Piper has reason to hesitate, as I'm sure you know about her past relationship. But she also hesitates to accept anything good that enters her life. It's in her nature. When she had her bat mitzvah, she questioned me for six weeks if the necklace I gave her wasn't too much. She has a kind heart, but make no mistake, she has a backbone and can be stubborn and confident when needed."

"Couldn't agree more. I'm just a little stuck, as my niece

wasn't thrilled with the news about Piper and myself, and I know it's keeping Piper down."

She waves off my notion. "April and Piper will find their way back to one another. Something will bring them together again."

I hum at the thought. "I think so too. Maybe I should do more, I've kind of stayed on the sidelines."

Her eyes stay fixed on me and don't blink. "As much as I'm sure my granddaughter's friendship suffering from her choice of gentleman suiter is a topic of discussion, I'm more interested in your mention of being a traditional guy."

I laugh, as she sees right through me. "Fair enough. I'm sure you've done your research on me, so I don't need to go over my backstory."

"Certainty have, and the media loves you, as do the women at my Tuesday-night book club."

"Fun." I move quickly on. "I just need you to know that my intentions are honorable, and I hope when the schedule allows, that we can have dinner together. Until then, I promise that I'll take care of Piper, always."

She lifts her nose and folds her hands over her skirt. "Sounds like some long-term plans."

"They are. I've made it clear to Piper what I want in life, and she's still around which tells me she thinks I'm a keeper." I tone down my cockiness for a second.

"You've kept her busy the last few months, that's for sure. I have a talent, they say. I can judge someone's character within ten seconds, and my thought about them will never change. Unlucky for many, but exceptionally lucky for Piper, as I'm never wrong."

The corners of my mouth twist while I wait for her to continue.

"I have a good feeling about you."

"Only good?" I joke.

"You would get an extra point if you tell me you have a Jewish grandfather or something, but meh."

I chuckle because her face is dead serious. "If I say I have every intention of making her my wife, would you still have a very good feeling about me?"

She wiggles her long finger in the air. "I don't change my opinions of people."

Ah, she agrees with me.

"You may think I'm moving fast, but I'm not getting any younger, and I live a life where my days revolve around a game that you always want to win. No room for error, nor opportunity to slow things down. So the moment that I put in the effort for something, then everything goes out the window. That's it, I want it until I have it. For the first time, I put in the effort with a woman, and it's because I can't imagine my life without her. I wouldn't even know how to let go if I tried, nor do I plan on stumbling either."

"You sound like Piper's grandfather. He had the same demeanor. Also, older than me and a smooth talker. I understand where you are coming from. It may scare Piper like crazy, but sometimes we need someone to take us out of our comfort zones, albeit in a positive way."

"Couldn't agree more."

In that moment, we hear the front door to the apartment open, and our attention turns to the entrance.

"They only had roast beef. Simon swears you didn't have an order in for this week," Piper announces as she juggles a bag and her purse. When she drops the bags and looks up, she stops in her tracks, and her mouth parts open in surprise. "Hudson?"

I stand to greet her. "In the flesh."

She slowly walks to me and looks between her grandmother and me, a nervous smile appearing on her face. "What are you doing here?" I hear the disbelief in her voice that she walked in on this surprise.

I'm quick to give her a kiss hello, far too chaste for my liking. "I had a little free time and thought I would introduce myself."

Piper's eyes have a hint of shock. "Oh, uhm, and you thought to take matters into your own hands?" I can't quite figure out if she's mad or entertained.

"See, Ruth, she is a smart woman this one." I play into the amused side.

Her grandmother focuses on Piper. "Relax, dear, we were having a good discussion. About you, of course, and we covered the essentials. I mean, I'm just going to assume his *package* is up to my standards."

Piper's face turns near white. "Oh my." She shakes her head and walks to the tray of alcohol. "This is why I was petrified of this scenario." She pours herself a decent drink.

"I didn't even do an inspection and my special sense told me that he's a keeper within ten seconds."

"What in the world is the inspection?" Piper looks petrified, but I can only laugh.

Her grandmother stands. "Well, I haven't asked, and I was kind of hoping, but you know what? I think I've given up that particular criteria, and being circumcised is more for your enjoyment than tradition, but it's fine. Besides, I have a feeling this guy would be the type of guy to ask for my input on wedding rings and maybe name my first grandchild after me, so we are good to go."

Piper takes a long gulp.

I walk to her and bring my hand to her upper arm. "Are you okay?"

"Of course she is, she has you in her life to take off those lacy pieces she designs."

Piper's mouth falls open again when she looks at her grandmother. "Tone it down." She looks at me. "It's not that I didn't want you to meet, I just know she has zero filter, and it requires like a few hours of mental preparation for dealing with you two in the same room."

I rub her shoulders. "And now you've had no mental preparation. I like the element of surprise."

"She's fine. She loves my candid honesty. It's more likely she was afraid that I might not like you and now she can relax because you have my seal of approval," her grandmother announces.

Her head perks up. "You like him?" Piper's voice turns soft, and her eyes fill with that familiar glimmer of hope and admiration that I've seen a few times now.

Her grandmother nods, and that's what it takes for Piper to relax and smile an honest smile.

"I'll give you two a minute while I do some things in the kitchen. And if you need *a moment,* just use the guest room at the end."

"Well, that's a special offer," I retort.

When Ruth is out of the room, Piper's head falls against my shoulder. "Are we not allowed any normal family meetings?"

"That wouldn't be fun."

Piper looks up at me, and I'm quick to cradle her face in the palms of my hands and kiss her soft and long until she's murmuring into my breath. I haven't seen her since the other week, and while she knew I was in the city, we didn't set a time in stone for when we would see one another.

"It's a busy time, and I wish I could stop the clock," I admit.

"Me too. I hate city life now, and I hate sleeping alone or at least not knowing the pillow next to me smells of you."

I kiss her forehead. "You can always stay in Lake Spark, even if I'm not there."

"I know. Maybe I will head there sometime in the coming weeks. I can focus on work, hang with the knitting ladies since April is still MIA from my life, and survive on coffee with jellybeans."

"Could be a solid plan."

Piper stares at me and her eyes flutter, and I know her soft playful voice is about to come on. "You should be in trouble for this move."

I pull her flush against my body and wrap my arms around her. "Sometimes you need a little push, and I wanted to be a little traditional."

"Should have done this before you spanked me in the bedroom then." That fucking sexy voice.

My brows raise from her boldness, and I pull her tighter against my body. "I'm a little late on that, but I can spank you harder next time."

She purrs into my neck and loops her arms around my neck, then she tilts her body against my dick. This woman is being a little vixen.

"Stay for dinner then we can leave together?" she offers.

"I wish, but I have a dinner with sponsors and won't finish until late. Football season isn't going to be on our side."

She sighs and nods in understanding. "I get it."

I crook my finger under her chin to tip her face up. "There are 168 hours in the week, of which about 115 of those hours are coaching and 35 for sleeping. I hope every sleeping hour you are next to me, and any hours left in the week are for you, but even so, it depends on where a game might be. But it doesn't matter, as you are always on my mind."

"I know. I'm getting used to it."

Piper's grandmother interrupts us. "You know if you marry, the coaches' wives have an association."

We both look at her, and she shrugs her shoulders.

"How much have you heard?" Piper wonders.

"Enough."

I scoff a laugh again. "You're something special, Ruth."

"I know." She doesn't hold in any modesty.

Looking back at Piper, I'm happy that we can strike another milestone off the list.

———

HOLDING my phone to my ear, I wait for my sister to pick up. My driver is getting me to my next location for the day, so I have some time to kill.

"Oh dear, what have you done now?" Catherine greets me on the other end.

"Love you too. Can't a guy call his sister?"

"You can, but you've been occupied lately. Speaking of which, I hear April is still giving you and Piper the silent treatment."

I look out the window where we are stuck at a traffic light during rush-hour traffic on the north side of Chicago.

"She is, but I'm hoping to rectify that, as Piper and I are not going to fade away. I was hoping they could sort it all out, but that doesn't seem to be happening, so I'm tapping in. I need your help."

Catherine hums. "You understand where April is coming from, right?"

"Partly, but not enough that it's an issue. Look, I know

she hasn't had the best of romantic endeavors lately, but even more reason why she could use her friend, and I need Piper happy too, especially now that she's losing me to the football season schedule. I'd feel better knowing she has her best friend back."

"For selfish reasons, you call, but luckily I love you, and you did promise that I could have a spa day at the Dizzy Duck Inn on your account—"

My body sits up in reaction. "That's it. You're a genius. See, I knew phoning you would be a good idea. Thanks!"

"Wait, what? What just happened? I'm confused."

"Gotta go, need to call April." I hang up and quickly dial April's number, even adding video.

I wait and wait, but eventually April answers.

"Yes?" I hear attitude which only makes me smile.

"You can't stay mad at me. We're family, and my son is connected to the best winery around and I coach your favorite team, so you need me."

She holds her hand up. "Oh, don't worry. Drew isn't getting my silent treatment since he didn't sleep with my best friend. Why did you, my cool uncle, have to become a cliché?"

"I'm not a cliché. I found a beautiful woman who I want to spend my life with, and she just so happens to be your age and your friend. I can't apologize—"

"I know. You have no problem staying firm on your stances. It's why you're a coach."

I smile at her thought. "I know somewhere in your smart head that if you look at it more, then you would understand. Anyways, it happened and here we are, and I just wanted to invite you to Lake Spark sometime soon for a spa day. I promised your mom it would be on me and thought I would extend the invitation."

April looks at me, intrigued yet doubtful.

"Will Piper be there?"

"No. Would it matter, though? I know you miss her. I mean, she misses you. Just the other day she was in a mood because she saw a dog and said it reminded her of you."

"Was it a beagle?" April nearly smiles.

I nod and see we are approaching our destination on all counts.

"Listen, I've got to run, but will you make it happen? Visiting Lake Spark?"

"I mean, I guess I can cram it into my busy schedule of ice cream, ripping up photos of my ex, and wondering where I went wrong in life."

I cringe at that thought. "How are you doing with that?"

"Swell," she says, sarcastic.

"You deserve so much better, and you will find someone."

"If I had a penny every time someone told me that, then, well, I would be swimming in coins."

I unbuckle my belt as the car comes to a standstill. "All the more reason to have a nice escape. Just send me your available dates."

"Fine."

"We'll be in touch," I say as the car door opens.

"Bye."

"Bye, kiddo."

Satisfaction spreads on my face because I have every intention of trapping April and Piper together, and I know they will thank me later. After that, we can just all move forward, because surely we've crossed every possible blip off the list.

22

PIPER

Hudson fixes his collar. We're sitting in the back of the car with his driver up front. Admittedly, I got a little handsy when we had a two-hour window. Between his meetings with team administration and the schedule of getting on a plane for an away game, this is what we get.

But it's okay because Hudson picked me up from my apartment. We drove around with the full intention of grabbing something to eat but got side-tracked.

Since the other week when he showed up at my grandmother's, something has swelled inside of me. To some, his move may have been a step too far, yet it felt perfectly right. Typical Hudson, too, as the man has zero patience except when it involves football. And he completely has my grandmother wrapped around his little finger. He had dressed to impress and spoke with honesty; it was enough to slay any woman's heart.

"You may want to straighten your blouse. I'm not a fan of other people gawking at your beautiful tits." He gives me a stern eye with a subtle smirk on his mouth.

I glance down to see my buttons are undone. "You've left me disheveled yet again."

Hudson angles his body toward me and slides his hand along my cheek. "Don't kill me for saying it but you seem different."

I work my buttons closed. "Oh? Well, work is a little crazy, I guess. I'm lucky that I outsource so many things and I rely on internet orders, but I really need to find a new spot to kind of set up base. I also had a hell of a week. I wasn't too thrilled with the model who showed up for a photoshoot for the spring collection, and I mean, April is still, well…"

"You're stressed."

I tip my head to the side in contemplation. "Maybe… a little." I'm missing a confidante in my life, in the shape of a best friend.

"I can tell. But I have just the thing to help. How about you drive up to Lake Spark for the weekend and have a spa day, your boyfriend's treat."

Curiosity floods my face. "That's quite an offer."

"When you go to Lake Spark, you're always occupied with me, which is a perfect way to enjoy Lake Spark, but the spa is one of the best."

I rub the back of his hand with my thumb and hold his wrist. "I mean, I guess a few days of calm would be good for me. I've worked at your house before, and I wouldn't complain about nabbing a coffee with jellybeans every day."

"It's settled then."

I lean in to kiss him on his lips. "Thank you." Because it's a sweet gesture, and I think he's noticed that I've been down since April made it clear she wasn't happy with how I handled my relationship with her uncle.

"I'm being selfish. I need to know that you're okay while I'm thousands of miles away."

The corner of my mouth tugs, and I move to straddle him and hook my arms around his neck, ensuring our eyes are locked. "Don't worry. I'm fine and as prepared as I can be for your mind to be in the game many hours of the day and the fact you need to focus. I promise to only send any inappropriate selfies after 10pm."

He playfully pinches my sides. "You'll be at one of the upcoming home games?"

I nod my head, but inside I feel my breath get caught because that means more eyes and cameras. "How about I send you a pre-game photo of what I'm wearing underneath my Winds t-shirt to keep you motivated?" I throw him a sexy look.

He growls before he kisses the base of my throat. "If you do that then I'll absolutely devour you later, take you to the edge, and leave you hanging. There will be consequences," he taunts me back.

"That's not a deterrent."

Hudson quickly looks out the window and sees that my drop-off is approaching. "Here we are. I hate this."

"You be safe. Get sleep and eat well. It'll be a good season," I assure him.

He smiles gently. "I like hearing you say that. It's refreshing to hear it from someone not trying to kiss my ass." His fingertips brush a loose strand of my hair behind my ear. "Actually, I like having someone to share this world with who isn't a sports person."

I kiss him again and pull my body tighter against him to hug with everything I have.

"Easy there," he warns me.

I giggle as the car stops, and I hop off his lap. My hand is on the door handle, even though I know the driver will open it. Hudson stops me. "Piper, what I was saying earlier about how you seem different..."

"Yes?" I look at him, puzzled.

The gentlest of closed-mouth smiles stretches on his mouth. "Still no birth control, right?"

I shake my head no.

He looks at me, waiting for me to catch on.

But it takes a little longer for my brain to connect. It's only when his eyes gawk at me that I understand.

"Oh."

Hudson reaches out with the back of his finger once more to rub my cheek. "Yeah, oh." He flashes his eyes. "It's the way I want it."

I know he hopes that I'm pregnant, but truthfully, it hasn't crossed my mind, as we're not actively trying, nor actively being safe either. We don't say anything else about the topic as we bid one another goodbye.

————

ARRIVING at the front desk of the spa, I'm occupied with tying my hair up into a messy bun. Nonetheless, the calming music does bring me down a smidgen on the stress scale, and the candles, green plants, and swinging chairs all set the tone that I've entered tranquil territory.

When Hudson suggested this the other week, I just kind of agreed to be polite. Well, staying at his house wasn't, I was honest that I focus well at his place, so I have no qualms about coming to Lake Spark while he's away, but a spa day is kind of special, and I figured it was something he was just suggesting to be nice. But Hudson doesn't suggest, he acts. So, a few days later, he told me that he'd booked me in at the Dizzy Duck Inn.

"Good morning, you must be Piper." The woman my age with impeccable skin greets me from behind the desk.

"Yeah, that's me. I have, or my boyfriend, he made a reservation for me." I'm still getting used to calling him that, but it makes a small smile break out.

The woman studies the screen with a welcoming look. "Indeed, he booked you quite a day. Full-body massage, facial, nails, and you also have a lovely lunch later on the terrace, and you can use the sauna and jacuzzi, of course. Can I get you some mint water to start? You are having a massage first."

My brows raise, as I'm impressed that Hudson arranged all of that, and wow, I am a lucky girl. "Water would be good."

"Sure. I will show you the changing room so you can throw on a robe, and I'll get you that water." She grabs a few folded towels from behind her on the shelf and indicates with her hand that I should follow her. "Your friend is here already."

"Friend?"

She glances over her shoulder. "Yes. The day is for two people... or did you not know that?" An awkward smile forms on her mouth.

I laugh under my breath before my lips roll in then quirk out because I should have seen this coming. Hudson isn't shy to do things. "Let me guess..."

She opens the door and in my full view is April tying her fluffy white robe. "Piper." April's voice fills with disdain, but even that feels more for theatrics.

The lady from the spa looks between us and manages to hold her smile. "I'll give you two a few minutes and get some water. When you're both ready, you have a partner massage in room three."

April and I don't take notice of the woman leaving, instead we stare at one another.

"I guess my mother isn't meeting me for a spa day… Sounds like typical Hudson." April crosses her arms.

I step into the changing room and walk to the hanging robe, not bothering to look at April. "Maybe I knew deep down that he would conspire to get us into a room together." I grab the robe.

"Right. Because you two are soul mates now." April's sentence is dripping with sarcasm, which causes me to throw a glare in her direction. Immediately, April seems to look remorseful. "Sorry," she clips. "But I'm not leaving."

"You don't need to," I say as I begin to undress.

"Good. Because I could use a spa day."

"Me too."

"Fine."

Silence takes over the room, and when I tie my robe, we seem to be in a stare-off. "We should probably head to our massage."

April lifts her head. "Okay, but if we get a hot masseuse, then obviously he's mine."

I shake my head. "No argument there."

I turn to put my phone in the locker, and I see Hudson is calling me on the screen, as my phone is on silent. I quickly answer and bring the phone to my ear. "Can't talk long, as the massage is about to start." I speak in a near-hushed tone.

"You're not going to kill me?" I can hear him grinning through the phone.

Looking at April, I smile tightly. "No. I… appreciate the deception."

"You're getting a spa day *and* your friend out of this, baby. I'm sure you will show your appreciation later." There is sinfulness in his tone, and it causes me to grow bashful.

"Now isn't the time for this discussion. I'm sure April won't kill me, I mean, as long as her masseuse is hot and single."

Hudson snorts a laugh. "Not a fucking chance. I made sure you have two women. I'm not having some guy stare at your fine body. I'd rip his head off, even if he is being professional. Nobody sees you naked but me."

Whoa, there is some possessiveness in his tone, the good kind. Well, bad, because I feel an effect between my legs and I'm now going for a massage.

"Okay, okay, we need to go. I'll phone you later. Good luck with your team meetings today." I quickly end the call.

April gives me a pointed look before pivoting to walk down the hall. I follow her and roll my eyes. I know it may take a little for her to warm up to me.

And during the massage, we made one step when I noticed a hint of entertainment when she realized she wouldn't be getting any good-looking spa men today, and she seemed relaxed like me when the massage was finished, even asked if I enjoyed mine.

Now we're sitting on rocking chairs with masks on our faces and overlooking the indoor water feature while sipping on cucumber water. As much as I have a bunch of questions so we can catch up, I'm waiting for her cues.

But then when I see her watching a small group of women leaving the changing room with pink satchels that indicates it's a bachelorette weekend, then I know what's occupying April's thoughts.

"I bet lunch will be delicious," I attempt to divert her attention.

April looks at me. "Ginger, it's okay, I'm not going to burst into tears."

Is this a step? She called me my nickname for the first

time in a long time. I give her a sympathetic look. "You don't need to get married to have a nice spa weekend."

"No. I just need a best friend who is sleeping with my rich uncle." Her tone and look are actually a relief because I know she was attempting to make a joke.

I try to hide my smile. "So, I'm still your best friend?"

April sighs and places her glass on the side table. "I have a right to be mad. You lied to me for months."

Setting my own glass down, I angle my body toward her. "I could have handled it differently, I know."

"And I'm a horrible person," she states.

"That should probably be my line in this situation."

April blows out another breath. "I think I was also mad because... you get to fall in love when my heart has been stepped on. What kind of friend doesn't want their friend to be happy?"

I reach out to touch her arm in comfort. "The kind of friend who is human and just had an engagement ripped away from them because the guy is an absolute tool, and even though it's for the best, it still stings."

"He is a tool. We were supposed to go to Italy on our honeymoon, and now I have to ditch those plans."

"You can still go. Maybe now you can do that cooking course instead of what he wanted to do."

April attempts to smile. "I guess I can get a dog now too since he was allergic."

I give her a knowing look. "But was he?" My voice raises to a near squeak. "Or was he just saying that because he doesn't like dogs?"

April laughs and tries to keep her tears back. "Fuck, the signs were there all along, weren't they? We weren't a match."

I shrug. "I don't know, I mean, opposites attract, so don't beat yourself up about that."

"Are you and Hudson opposites?" she wonders.

I take hold of my drink again to occupy myself, as I'm not sure how to talk to her about my boyfriend who happens to be her uncle and godfather. There are some topics that may be a little too uncomfortable to discuss, I'm aware of that.

"In some ways, sure. He's all or nothing, determined, focused yet laid back. I'm… laid back, focused, and hesitant with many things in life. So maybe we meet in the middle."

"Are you hesitant about him?" April asks point blank.

A warm smile comes naturally. "I feel different when I'm with him. From the moment that I met him, actually. I've always done slow, and he does… fast. But it's okay, as I feel safe and free. That was something I didn't think I would ever feel again in a relationship."

This time April reaches out to touch my shoulder. "He is by far the furthest thing from your douchebag of an ex."

"I know. I don't think that really comes into play, it's more the feelings in general. But I'm not sure I'm coach's-wife material, I mean the whole in-the-spotlight thing."

"First-world problems, I guess. But just be yourself. It isn't about you in those moments. I don't see my uncle often because he's married to his career, maybe not even by choice. Being head coach just takes a lot of hours, but for the first time he wants to attempt to be tied to something outside of football. It just so happens to be my friend."

Our eyes meet, and perhaps this is our turning point. "It really sucked not being able to share things with you."

"I know the feeling."

"Can we move forward?" My voice is hopeful.

April seems to contemplate. "I've wallowed for weeks. Maybe I needed the time to digest the news about you and my uncle too. I think we can move forward... but if you and my uncle don't work out, then it might be awkward, so I guess that means... you need to work out." There's a humorous undertone. "And I know lingerie is your career, but maybe let's put a pin in those discussions, or at least don't add my uncle's name into the same sentence."

"I can live with that." I nod.

"I guess it only took a massage and facial to get us to talk. I was kind of expecting we would at least need the pedicure too before we really talked," she quips.

"I'm happy we're ahead of schedule then because I've really missed having a best friend in my life," I admit. "I have so much to share, and I was so worried about you."

"I could use my friend back too."

The corners of our mouths curve up and tears form in our eyes before we lean in to hug one another, then tears actually burst out. "I'm so sorry."

"Me too."

We squeeze tighter in our hug, careful not to make a mess of our face masks.

The spa attendant comes to interrupt us to take our masks off, and just in time, as I feel my face cracking.

"Oh God, are we going to get weird lines on our faces because we cried with this magical mud on?" April wonders.

The attendant smiles. "Believe it or not, you two are not the first to cry while in the mask. You should be fine. Some even say the tears enhance the experience."

April and I look at each other and burst out laughing.

———

Now back in normal clothes, I arrive at our table overlooking Lake Spark. It's clear blue skies today.

April looks up from her phone. "They offered us a high tea with little sandwiches and cakes, but I changed it to burgers and fries."

"Oh, thank God." I'm relieved that she knows me so well. "I feel like that massage was like running a marathon. Or maybe it was the sauna, but I'm starving."

"I guess you are all up-to-date on Lake Spark, so did you go to Jolly Joe's or Catch 22?"

I nod as I sip from my iced tea. "It feels like a second home almost. Just kind of sucks that Hudson is now in foot-ball season so won't be here much."

"It sounds like you will, though. Moving in?" she asks simply.

I laugh. "No. Well, it's more like my apartment in the city is a place where I sleep and here it feels like... a home."

She raises a brow at me. "That's promising."

"Actually... there is this little boutique on Main Street. Apparently, it's been empty for a while, but the family didn't want to sell. I saw a sign go up today that it's for sale." Excitement comes out in my words because it would be great spot for Piper Ginger.

April studies me for a second then grins. "Exactly what Lake Spark needs, a classy lingerie company."

I wave my hand. "It's just a silly thought."

"No, it's not." She looks over my shoulder. "Ooh, I see our food arriving."

A few moments later, with food in front of us, April checks her phone for a moment. "That dress is stunning by the way," she mentions.

"What dress?"

"The one you were wearing when you were packing on the PDA with Coach Arrows."

My face turns bewildered, as I don't understand, and

April notices, so she shows me her phone. "You're online. One of the players' wives posted a video from practice and someone pointed out what they saw in the background… you and my uncle."

I look at the screen, and my stomach sinks because there I am in Hudson's arms. It looks innocent enough, but very much makes the message clear that I'm his significant other. "Oh, I didn't know about this. We were going to announce when we were ready with a photo of coffee mugs or a view of a sunset or something like that."

April snorts a laugh and takes her phone back, scrolling frantically. "Well, a little late for that. You are an entire hashtag. Oh, 'arrow to his heart,' that's a cute comment. Actually… you and my uncle are kind of blowing up the internet." She tilts her head to the side. "Ooh, I see we have a few new articles. 'Coach Arrows is no longer a bachelor!' There is also 'This is the year for Coach Arrows on and off the field.'"

"What?" I feel a sense of panic come over me. A waiter walks by, and I quickly signal for him to stop. "Can I have martini?" My head is spinning, but just as quickly as I requested the drink, I backtrack. "Wait! Can I just have… a Shirley Temple maybe."

April's eyes blaze open and her mouth drops. "Holy shit. You just turned down alcohol."

I breathe out a long calming exhale and hold my palm up. "It's not what you think."

23

PIPER

I throw another bar of chocolate into our shopping basket while April appears with two bottles of wine in hand. I give her a skeptical look.

"You know what I love about the Lake Spark general store? It's like a grocery store from the city, with an abundance of quality wine choices. I don't think there is one single bottle of crap wine on the shelf here. And I can't decide if it's a rosé or straight-up white wine kind of night. Are you sure you don't want any vino right now?" she double-checks.

I shake my head and confidently offer her the basket. "I need a clear mind."

At the spa it took a solid few minutes to convince April that I'm not pregnant, even when I explained that I really just want to be able to think clearly this weekend and was feeling the effects of the massage. I convinced April to ditch her night at the inn and stay at Hudson's since he's away anyways.

He texted that he would call when he was done with team meetings because he saw the video of us online, to which his response was, "*Damn it, should have had my hand on your ass for the extra wow factor.*"

We turn down the next aisle and nearly run into Spencer, Hudson's neighbor. "Oh, hey there, ladies," he greets us, and I notice immediately how his eyes land on a glaring April.

"Hey!" I look between them then brush past it. "I was hoping to run into you, as I think you've been collecting the packages of materials I had delivered, and you left them by the back door. I wanted to thank you."

"Yep. That's me."

"He's a real saint, I'm sure." April's tone is pure snark.

This is one weird vibe happening. "So, uhm, I guess you're around more now that baseball season is over?" I attempt to make conversation.

Spencer turns his attention to me. "I am. Just give me a shout if you need something. Hudson texted to let me know you would be around more and then mentioned something about the pine tree or some shit like that."

"Yeah, he has this annoying tree." Silence fills our bubble, and I'm not entirely sure April or Spencer realize I'm still here, but they both look like they may kill one another. "Right. So April and I should probably head back to the house. Beat the weekend fox rush on the road, you know."

Silence.

I grab April's arm. "Okay, bye."

"Bye, ladies!" Spencer calls out.

April and I approach the register, and I let her arm go and look straight at her. "Explain."

"He's an asshole. I met him once when my uncle had a BBQ, and he was at my cousin Drew's wedding. Every time he talks, I want to bang my head against a wall. He just constantly brags about his success." She pretends to gag.

"Well, he's nice enough to me."

"Lucky you."

I shake my head and focus on our turn at the register.

A few minutes later, we're back outside and ready to load my car, but I stop when I notice the for sale sign on the empty store for the second time today, a reminder of my crazy thought.

April looks in the direction of my sight. "You're really considering it, aren't you?"

I smile and shrug it off shyly. "Nah, it's crazy."

"Is it, though? Your living room became your warehouse, so I guess if you were looking to move away from the city then this is a sign."

"Real estate isn't that cheap here."

April's eyes grow big. "You have some money saved, a growing business, a rich grandmother, and an even richer boyfriend. You're good."

I laugh at her absurdity and get into the car. Yet the image of the for sale sign doesn't leave my mind on the way to the house.

———

SITTING on the edge of the bed, I hold my phone up as Hudson graces the screen.

"You're lying in bed, aren't you?" I flash my eyes at him.

"I am. I'm a little beat."

My lips quirk. "You'll get a good night of sleep and anni- hilate those Cougars tomorrow."

"Would be a better night of sleep if you were here."

"Ah, don't go soft on me, Coach." I lean back on the bed, and to tease him, move my shirt slightly off my shoulder. "Besides, I need to behave because your plan worked and now April and I are having a night in with snacks and movies."

Hudson smiles proudly. "I'm a smart man."

"You're annoying," I joke. "You make things happen."

"I do have talents," he quips. "So, about that video. Smith's wife apologized and also asked the engagements coordinator for your number to send an apology. She didn't realize her error. But really, it's no big deal, right? I mean, now we don't have to spend ten minutes trying to figure out if our coffee mugs have the right light for a photo."

I laugh. "True that. It's not a big deal. I mean, we knew it was coming, she just put us a little ahead of schedule." We were going to post something after the next home game.

"I got questioned during press rounds this afternoon, so you may want to watch that."

"Ooh, now I'm curious."

He throws an arm behind his head. "You'll be at the next home game, right?"

"Oh." I bite my bottom lip because I feel a pool of doubt in my belly. Fears resurface of people's opinions and uncertainty over whether I'm moving too fast. "I'm not completely sure," I admit. The comments I saw on the latest article seemed to emphasize that I'm a trophy. Never mind the fact that I run a successful business, I'm now a glorified doll.

"What do you mean?" I hear disappointment in his voice.

"It's a lot of press, and I'm not entirely sure I feel up to it energy-wise."

Now he looks at me, confused. "What does that mean?"

"My mind is a little overloaded right now, and I haven't slept so great. Can I see how I feel at the end of the week?" I say it before even thinking it over.

But Hudson's disapproval is apparent on his face.

"Piper... I'm going a little crazy on the merry-go-round of hot-cold-hot. I need to know that you're on board with this life. I can't make it disappear. So yes, being with me means you are probably going to have to get out of your comfort zone more than you are accustomed, because I want to be with someone who *wants* to be at my games and there for me, not dragged along."

I hold my hand up. "I don't think we should talk about this now. You're tired, and April is downstairs."

"No, we're not going to talk about this now. In fact, I don't want to talk about it until you've thought this all through and have made a decision that you're comfortable with. As much as I love you, you're bringing out an uneasiness that I haven't felt in years."

Shit. I'm ruining this, but he's right, and I need to clarify my standpoint and thoughts before we discuss it further.

"You're right," is all I can say.

And just like that, we have our first fight.

———

I THROW the remote for the fireplace to the side and look at April who is studying me intently while she pours herself a glass of wine at the coffee table in Hudson's living room.

"It's kind of weird seeing you in this habitat. It's like you are the lady of the house."

I snort a laugh. "What in the world does that mean?"

She takes a sip of her wine. "You know where everything is, walk around like it's your home, and seem calm here. I'm going to assume most of your romantic rendezvous with my uncle took place here, so that explains it, I guess."

My jaw flexes side to side. "Your thought process might

be on point. And yes, I feel at home here, whether Hudson's here or not."

"That's a big deal."

I shrug it off and instead glance at the television that is mounted on the wall and that we put on pause. "Is it bad if I watch it again?"

April smiles at me. "Kind of sickly cute."

I press the rewind button, with guilt plaguing me. Pressing play, Hudson appears on the screen in the clip that he mentioned from earlier. It's the sports channel that I've gotten used to watching in recent months. I know they always have media following the team around while in season and today one of the reporters stopped Hudson after practice.

On the screen, Hudson is in jeans and a long-sleeved shirt with the team logo. He folds his arms as he listens to the man with the mic ask a question. "Everyone is counting on a win this week, but the Cougars have a strong defense from what we've seen this season. How are you feeling about tomorrow's away game?"

Hudson's face remains stoic, with a hint of cocky confidence twisting on the corner of his mouth. "My guys have been practicing hard and continue to study the plays, whether we need to have a strong offense or defense tomorrow. We also have a lot of new blood on the team this year, and I'm confident that they will bring some fresh energy to the game to support some of the best returning players in the industry that have come back this year."

"Would you say you're not going to lose sleep tonight about tomorrow's game?" The man with the mic returns the device to Hudson so he can speak.

"Nah. Only coaches who don't have confidence in their guys lose sleep."

The commentator laughs. "Fair enough. There is also a

rumor, thanks to a recent video, that you're now sharing your life with someone off the field. Care to comment?"

Hudson's grin is now uncontrollable, yet it's so incredibly suave. "My personal life has no effect on tomorrow's game, but it's true that I can now say life is better when you know there's someone waiting for you after a winning game, and I'm lucky that it's Piper."

"Will she be at your home game next week?"

"Whether Piper is there or not, I'm sure she'll be wearing a Winds shirt wherever she is." Hudson looks at the camera, and I swear every woman in America may just melt from that glint in his eye that feels like a secret message only for me, yet the female population's minds may be running wild.

I turn the television off, and I know I have a silly look on my face.

"Geez, no pressure or anything. My uncle really knows how to lay it on thick, right?"

Rolling my eyes, I sigh. "A tad. He likes to get what he wants, I guess. It's kind of endearing, and I'm maybe an idiot for thinking that."

"Nah, he takes care of you. Maybe now I can go to games with you and we can find me a hot sports guy. Before Hudson would never introduce me to anyone, but maybe you can soften his stance for me. I mean, you did draw me a wedding dress that I'll need to use one day." April crosses her legs, with her feet resting on the sofa.

I'm kind of surprised she brought up the dress. "I'll keep the design for you."

"Can I look at it?"

My eyes narrow. "Is that a good idea?" I ask, doubtful.

She sighs. "It's fine."

It takes a second before I search on my phone for the folder with the design. I debate if I'm only fueling April's misery, but she seems content with her request. Handing her my phone, I watch her study the screen.

"Boho chic, fitted yet comfortable, even has hidden pockets," I list. "I went for floor length, and the elements of lace are more traditional."

"It's beautiful." She sounds wistful.

"Thanks. It's not my forte, but the inspiration was there."

April hands me my phone and a knowing smirk forms. "I would have loved to have this dress, but you know… this is more your dress than mine."

"What?"

April nods her head. "That's right. You designed your own wedding dress."

I scoff at her thought. "No, I didn't."

Her facial expression turns goofy. "Uhm, yes, you did. Where did you get the inspiration for traditional lace?"

"My grandmother's dress." The S slurs. "Oh."

April laughs. "I remember you once told me when we were at your grandmother's for dinner that you would want to use some of the lace from her dress on your own wedding dress one day."

"And?"

April sets her wine glass back on the coffee table. "The dress. Your housewife skills. The boutique that caught your eye in Lake Spark for your future shop. Sounds to me like you've been setting all the puzzle pieces in place to make a life with someone. You did that because you found the right someone, and your heart knew it before your head."

"That's some theory." But the realization hits me like a ton of bricks, and I feel emotions running through me but in a way that is pure elation. "He is kind of angry at me right now because I keep taking a step forward, then step back. He wants me at his game, and I said maybe."

Her expression turns pained. "Yeah... probably not a smooth move on your part. He's never had a woman at a game, and now he's asked you. It's a big deal because he's laser-focused during a game."

"Even more reason for me to be slightly scared. People will have their eyes on me because it's unusual for Hudson."

"It's not about you. No offence, but as your newly reunited friend then I'm going to highlight that you're being a fool. The only opinion you should care about is the one you and my uncle have of each other. You know that too."

I run through my history in my head and know she has a solid point. The hesitation I have is unlike me because I've grown into a confident woman over the years.

"I know it's crazy, but I love him, and even though we are newish, I feel it in my bones that we are right. Maybe I thought it was lust and it would fade, but it's like we've been slowly building something profound together. It's just happening *already*."

"You two happened faster than some, but that's all the more reason why you maybe didn't realize it until now, when your extremely smart friend highlighted her brilliant ideas." She brings her hand to her heart with pride.

A smile tugs on my lips. "I probably should get it together, huh?"

April tips her wine glass to my direction. "Yep." She pops the P.

———

THE NEXT MORNING, I'm sitting outside and watching the sunrise with a mug of coffee in hand. I pull my knees up on the chair and one hand wraps my sweater tighter around my body.

There are exactly two things that I need to figure out before I talk to Hudson. It was during the night that I realized what those two things are. It may take a few days, but maybe the space will be good for us. We've been on a rollercoaster the last few months anyhow.

24

HUDSON

I grin when I see my son standing at my office door. One of the coordinators is standing at a distance to give us a bit of privacy, but not venturing far because I only get a few moments with Drew. In principle, players and staff don't see family or friends before a game, as I want the team focused. But it's still two hours until game time and my son is the exception. He is a calming necessity.

Holding out an arm, I give him a side hug. He has never been one for hugs, but I can tell it's growing on him, as his smile can't be hidden.

"I'm happy you're here."

Drew seems to brush it off. "A free ticket is a free ticket," he jokes.

"Yeah, yeah, yeah." I wave him off. "Sorry Lucy couldn't come." She wanted to help one of her brothers with the kids while her sister-in-law visits her parents.

"It's fine. Plus, I kind of assumed Piper would be here, so I won't be alone." He takes a seat on one the chairs while I perch at the edge of my desk.

Piper. The woman who drives me crazy and makes me constantly wonder if my love for her is infatuation in overdrive. But the truth is, I get the best of both—lust mixed with love. There is no doubt that I want her in my future because she is all I see when I think about it. Which makes her proclamation that she might not come to an important part of my career a bigger blow. It's a letdown to say the least.

I scratch my chin and wonder what to say without painting Piper in a bad light. "I'm not sure she'll be here."

"It's a big home game." He looks at me oddly.

I can only nod, roll my lips in, and say nothing.

"I don't particularly want to get into my dad's romantic life, but since it seems to be weighing on your mind, all okay with you two kids?"

My eyes give him a warning, because I think he may still have doubts about Piper. "She isn't feeling so great," I lie. Now my son returns the look that I gave him less than ten seconds ago. "Okay, I don't think she's coming."

Drew's eyes grow big, and he slides his thumb along his jaw. "So, there is a little trouble in paradise," he states more than asks.

"I wouldn't say that. I think Piper just needs to wrap her head around a few things. What, I'm not entirely sure, but she'll figure it out."

"It may not bode well for you." He highlights that fact.

I sigh and play with a pen that's lying on the desk. "Can't think about that now, it's game day."

"Ah yes, your brain compartmentalizes, an Arrows gene. Sometimes you forget that not everyone thinks the same way."

"Oh boy, my son showed up a wiseass today." A cheeky grin forms on my mouth.

"What?" He seems offended yet smirks. "Some people think in boxes, others don't. But that's not even the problem. You have zero patience. It's all or nothing, and because you have no patience, you try and get what you want at record speed."

I hold a finger up. "Wait a second. Are you trying to make an excuse for Piper? Are you on her team?"

He tilts his head to the side. "Anybody who sits through a dinner after what went down in your kitchen when I walked in gets a point from me. If she hesitates now with your relationship but figures out that you're for her, then I get where she might be coming from because we both know that you already have it in your head what kind of ring you might buy her. But if she can't figure it out or hesitates too much, then yeah, I think you should walk away."

I stand when I see one of the coordinators hold up his wrist to indicate time, but a hint of a smile doesn't fade from my lips. Not because of Piper, hell no, her not coming to the game would be a letdown and the mere thought has me wanting to throw a tantrum. My smile is for my son who just turned the table on me because a year ago I was dishing out romantic advice to him and now he's returning the favor... because he cares.

Drew stands, and I pat his shoulder. "I hear you, okay? You're going to stay at my place in the city tonight or drive back?"

"Not sure, depends if you guys lose or not."

"There is only one option for my guys." I'm a little cocky. "Go steal some food from the press box before you head to your seat," I remind him.

"Ah, you remember the only reason why I came," he jokes.

I shake my head and guide him to the hall by the shoulder. "Get out of here, kid."

Pausing for a second as I watch him walk off, I think about Piper and what Drew said. A twinge of understanding hits me, but not for long, as I need to focus on the upcoming game.

———

I'M ready to kill my quarterback, as his concentration seems to be lost. But we have enough time on the clock to get us the last point which would take us over the edge. It rained earlier, which will only make this messier.

"He seems in better position," I hear my assistant coach say in my headphones, as he's up in the press box over-looking the field.

Nodding to myself, I keep my focus on the field in front of me and stand firm in my spot. To many, I may appear calm and collected, but inside, I know I have a lot on the line if the last-minute play change is a miss. I would feel better knowing Piper was here, or rather if the agitation that she didn't want to come didn't have a firm spot inside of me, but I have to ignore it right now because I'm in coach mode.

I don't even look at the clock, just keep my attention on my quarterback who is calling out a play for the scrimmage line. We have twenty yards to go, and we can do it.

It's always the same, the last minute of a game. A blur. At the speed of light, someone may kick or run a pass, anything is possible to get the final point.

There isn't much more I can do, and I know I already have to mentally prepare for a post-game talk with the team and a press conference.

Relief hits me when I hear a ref say touchdown, and a whistle is blown to end the game. Immediately, I have assistant coaches slapping my back and players running to congratulate one another. I rub my face with my hand, suddenly relaxed. Post-game after a win is by far ten times better than a loss.

It's a round of handshakes with the opposing team's coaches and players, and a few of my team's guys too before I notice.

My smile changes to pure love.

Piper is standing on the sidelines, a perfect image. Fitted jeans, one of my team sweatshirts, and pink high heels. I make no mistake that they are the ones from the night we first met. A badge hangs around her neck that allows her to be here on the field. She wiggles her fingers in a cute little wave, and her closed-mouth smile tells me that she is unsure what to do yet satisfied that she caught me by surprise.

I pick up my pace and walk to her, quick to loop an arm around her middle and pull her to me.

"You're here." I speak loud enough for her to hear as the noise from the stadium fills our ears.

Now she smiles brightly. "I wouldn't miss it."

"But you said you—"

She shakes her head. "Now isn't the time to get into that. You just won, and I have no idea who can hear into that headset around your neck," she amusingly points out.

I chuckle. "God, you're here."

She glances away. "Kind of a perk of being your girl-friend. I get a free ticket." Her eyes turn back to me, this time with seriousness.

I look over her shoulder and see Drew giving us space and pretending not to watch us.

"He didn't give you a hard time, did he?"

Piper snickers. "It was a rough few minutes of convincing

him I was here with good intentions. He thawed when I offered to get a round of beers, and when I admitted to him that I made a mistake, then I think he finally gave me your signature smile."

I want to press her on the fact she just said that she admitted to making a mistake, but this just isn't the place. Instead, I rub her back.

Her mouth parts open to speak. "I shouldn't have let you doubt if I would be here or not. I know how much this means to you, so I *wanted* to be here. Actually, there is a lot I want, and I can't wait to tell you."

Her answer slays me, and I slide my hand through her hair to bring her face to me so I can cover her mouth with my own for a quick kiss that won't raise too many eyebrows.

I step closer to her, casting a protective touch to her elbow, aware that there are cameras everywhere. I lean in to speak so only she can hear. "I wish I could kiss you like crazy right now, but I have to talk to my guys and then face the press. Plus, I should probably review the video of the game while it's fresh in my head since that's what they pay me millions for."

She nods her head in understanding. "I figured. But I happen to know it's bye week, so you get a little break soon. Can we hold out until then?"

"Shit. I hate to say it, but we have no choice. By the time I'm out of here, I'll only get a few hours of sleep, then I'm back with my coaching staff."

The back of her hand runs along my jawline. "What's forty-eight hours more then, right?"

I scoff a laugh, look away, and then back to Piper. "Knowing there seems to be a promising conversation at the end of the wait, then yeah, we can do a grueling forty-eight hours." I take her hands in mine to give her fingers a quick squeeze with my own.

"It's *very* promising." Her eyes grow bold, and her closed-mouth smile insinuates that my patience may just pay off.

25

HUDSON

Truthfully, while players get to head home and be with their loved ones for a few days, I know I don't get to enjoy bye week the same way. Sure, my schedule is a little lighter than normal, but I will still need to strategize the season so far.

At least I get to head to Lake Spark, and I know Piper is already there, as she headed up first thing in the morning since she was already on the north side of the city to see her grandmother.

Arriving at my house, I open my car door and take a deep breath of lake air. The leaves are falling, and it's been a few weeks since I've been here. I'm happy Piper is keeping the house alive in my absence.

When I arrive inside the house, it's quiet. I know Piper is here, though, because she sent me a text, and I can tell she had a coffee in the kitchen.

"Piper?" I call out her name.

I drop my small bag on the ground and throw my keys onto the side table before I nearly jog up the stairs to my room.

Arriving at my bedroom door, I stop in my tracks when I see that Piper is sleeping peacefully on top of the blankets with one leg hooked over a pillow and her arms splayed over her head. Her heels are on the floor next to the bed. The light from the windows makes it clear that it's the middle of the day, which makes it all the more amusing that she fell asleep, because she doesn't nap.

Slowly, I approach my bed and the corners of my mouth tug just as my hand lands on her back to give her a soothing stroke. The mattress dips when I sit next to her. As much as I don't want to wake her… I need to. Our conversation can't exactly wait.

She must sense my presence, as she begins to slither in her spot, a groggy noise escaping her mouth.

"Hey there, sleepyhead."

Her eyes flutter open, then she adjusts to the fact I'm in front of her. The moment she registers that I'm here, she sits up.

"I must have dozed off." She yawns and stretches her arms over her head, causing her shirt to rise and her belly button to be on show. "Crap." Her hand comes to her forehead. "I was planning on surprising you with something new."

My brows knit together. "New collection new?" I'm hopeful.

"Something like that. I think we've established I'm not really good at timing surprises."

I swoop her hand into my own. "It's okay."

Her eyes connect with mine, and after a beat, she begins to speak. "Hudson, I'm sorry if I've been out of sorts, or rather cautious of a lot of things."

"I don't want you to feel like you have doubts."

She squeezes my hand. "The thing is, I don't have doubts.

I know that because it seems my life has been slowly inter-weaving with your own. I've been setting up the stepping-stones this whole time. I just needed to think clearly and realize that."

Her words are confident and everything to me. I kiss her hand like a gentleman would, but make no mistake, my plan to show her my satisfaction with her words is aligned with the brain of a dirty sailor.

"How did you realize it?"

She smiles shyly at me because she knows I like when she says it. "I'm insanely in love with you."

"What a coincidence, because I feel the same."

"That's good because I've kind of decided that I'm going all in on a future with you. I know I want to be waiting for you at every opportunity, and by chance, the old suit shop went on sale, so I decided to phone a realtor and make an offer. I don't know if I'll get it, but I gave it my best shot."

I can't control the approval flooding my face. "That's… great." It's commitment that she wants her life here with me.

"I think so. I could really make it a boutique and base for all my online orders. Plus, an endless supply of coffee from Jolly Joe's across the street. And an easy commute home, because that's what it feels like. Here, I mean, with you. Home." I love her words. They thrill me, and it unlocks the chains that have me trying to sit here politely and listen.

I pat her arm with my hand, an indication that she needs to scoot over. But side by side is not going to happen, I need to be between her legs with her eyes on me as I drive myself inside of her.

I coax her thighs open and walk my arms forward and swing my legs up onto the bed until I'm between her legs, with my head resting on her stomach.

"It's not easy. I know that. But I wouldn't have let us

continue if I didn't think you had it in you to be by my side," I admit.

She rakes her fingers through my hair. "You take care of people, guide people, but right now, let me do that for you."

"I'm not used to that, believe it or not. Leading the way is more my style."

"Oh, gee, I hadn't noticed."

I grab hold of her shirt with my teeth and pull it up for a tease before releasing the fabric.

She laughs. "What in the world is in your hair?" Her fingers seem to grab something from a few strands, and we both inspect it when she holds it up into the air.

Pine needles.

"It's that fucking tree by the driveway," I groan.

"Ah yes, killer pinecones and needles." She tosses the needle to the side.

I lift my body onto my forearms because we both have a task to do.

"Take it off, Piper." I hear the desire in my voice.

We both take everything from the waist down off. Slow and sweet will be for later.

I get a glimpse of her lace panties that were just flung to the floor and then give Piper a curious look. "I have full intention to check if you're wearing a matching bra later, but right now…" I touch her clit with my finger and feel that she is already soaking onto my fingers. "My focus is on being inside of you." I align myself and cradle her head in my hand, with my thumb planted on her bottom lip.

Her body tilts up when I slide into her, the sensation of me going deeper causing us both to moan and our lips to collide. For some reason, this feeling is more intense than usual.

I look at her mouth when I pull away and a sultry smirk

begins to form on her swollen lips. "Keep going. Ruin me. Ruin me for other men." God, her playful tone slays me.

"Baby, I did that the first night I laid eyes on you."

Our eyes hold as I slam into her again and again, her legs tightly wrapping around my waist, offering herself to me, and I take every piece she'll give.

And lucky for me, she gives it all.

———

I LOOK DOWN at the eggs in the pan, going for over easy today. The autumn sun is illuminating the kitchen, a solid track is playing on the Bluetooth, and the smell of coffee is strong. I told Piper to let me sleep in, as it will be my only chance as we head into the rest of the season, but I'm not made for long mornings in bed and still woke before her.

Glancing up from the sizzling of the skillet, I notice Piper straightening her hoodie and searching for her car keys

"What are you doing?"

She ignores me as she grabs her sunglasses. "Going into town for something."

"You look like you're trying to go undercover or something."

She freezes, her hand on the keys, and she peers up to stare directly at me. "Because... I don't want to be noticed."

"It's Lake Spark, nobody cares." I grab my coffee mug and indicate that there's a spot next to me. Taking a sip with one hand, I hold out my other arm to invite her to join me.

"Maybe I need to get something without anyone catching wind, and I was going to go first thing, but I slept in, Coach."

I chuckle under my breath. Every time she calls me that I know she is going to say something to surprise me.

"I know I haven't lost my touch if you're worn out after a night like last night."

We didn't really leave the bed, except for some dinner downstairs when I whipped up some pasta and pesto with chicken. We talked about what she'll do if she gets the shop on Main Street, what my schedule looks like in the coming weeks, which games she will be at, which dinner with sponsors, and what she can expect. All the things that we talked about before but this time she is committed. She'll even meet me at some away games, which is an effort since she can't travel with me due to team rules but can stay in my room at away games.

Slowly she walks to me. "Uh-oh. You have John Mayer on and you're wearing an apron to cook eggs?"

"I know you like it." I look down at my *This coach has a foul mouth and a big heart* apron. "Don't divert the topic. Again, what's with the outfit?"

She ignores my comment and approaches me tactfully. "So, I'm going to come at you from the blindside here."

"Ooh, she's talkin' football," I tease her.

Her wry smile stays stoic.

I turn the element off and move the pan to a cooler spot on the stovetop. "So, what's the deal? Why do you need to head to town?"

"The thing is, I wanted to do the whole buying property, moving into your home without asking, showing up to games thing for the right reasons, and even though they are risks, it's okay because I want it all and knew it would be okay. And since I'm confident with all the possibilities that could happen, then I think I need to address another elephant in the room…"

I'm not catching on. "As in?" I rest my hands on her shoulders, soothing her.

Her unusual look doesn't change. "We haven't been careful." I don't respond until her eyes bug out.

"No complaints," I answer.

The remnants of a smirk on her lips inform me she thought I would say that. "I thought I wasn't pregnant, even took a test the other week. For some reason I don't know, I was kind of disappointed but also thought it was for the better, so I could make all these decisions without a baby being part of the equation. Last night I went to sleep knowing that I had confirmed my future with you, and we talked about it yesterday. Everything feels right."

"What are you saying?"

"My body kind of did this weird thing where it felt the need to gag at the thought of toothpaste, and then I realized I lost the box with the second test, so now I need to sneak around and buy another…" she rambles.

I feel my heart pounding. "Wait… hold up."

Piper takes a deep breath. "I'm not sure that test was correct, because it was maybe too early, so I need to take another one," she clarifies.

I blink a few times then something clicks me into action mode. "I'll go."

She doesn't get a chance to protest and two minutes later I'm back in the kitchen grabbing my car key. Piper never left her spot.

"Hudson!" she scolds me.

"What?"

Her eyes assess me up and down. "Did you not get the memo about being on the down-low for this outing?"

I give myself the once-over and realize my error. I'm literally wearing a hoodie that says Coach Arrows, not exactly subtle.

"Solid point." I guess I'm a little nervous. "I'll go change."

Piper shrugs. "Just, I don't know, buy a few things, then maybe nobody will notice. Like literally walk down the aisle and grab a box like a football pass, you don't even need to stop."

"I've totally got it covered," I assure her. "How about you just eat some breakfast and I'll be back before you know it."

She nods nervously, and I kiss her forehead.

Fifty-three minutes, a cinnamon roll pick-up, and a diversion of one morning fox later, I find myself staring out my bedroom door to the balcony and turning my head when I hear the bathroom door click open. I'm calm, though definitely excited at the prospect too.

Piper's face is unreadable. She takes one step closer.

"And?"

Piper's face erupts into a wide grin. "Looks like you're going to be a dad again."

My heart swells right before the reminder sinks in that I missed the young years with Drew, so this is just as new for me as it is Piper. I reach out and grab her wrists to pull her into my arms.

"The baby has good timing too, as he or she should arrive just on time in the middle of off-season." Tears form in her eyes, the good kind, because her mouth is stretched into a ridiculous grin.

I cup her cheek with the palm of my hand. "You really know how to make me happy, huh?" She nuzzles into my hand, the lids of her eyes closing. "We're getting married tomorrow."

Her head perks up. "W-what?"

"I'm not wasting time. You're having my baby, and there is only one way that I want this to go."

She scoffs at me, but her face says she's entertained. "We can't get married tomorrow. You can't even legally arrange it that quick unless we go to Vegas, and no, I'm not going to Vegas." She gives me a warning glare.

"We can get a license at the county clerk's office in the morning and then Pete can marry us."

"The owner of Jolly Joe's?"

"Yeah, he's a retired judge... the candy shop is a retirement hobby."

Piper blinks her eyes several times. "Oh... you're serious about everything you said in the last minute?"

I pull her tight then lift her up onto the dresser, setting a hand on each side of her body. "Of course I am."

Her fingers play with the tie of my hoodie that does not say coach. "I know you are." She kisses the corner of my mouth. "And lucky for me, I don't want to take the risk of you losing your patience, otherwise a wedding cake will magically appear anyway."

I kiss her forehead and interlace our hands. "Is that a yes you will marry me then?"

"Is this the proposal?" She cocks an eyebrow at me.

"Not even the beginning," I promise.

EPILOGUE: PIPER

ONE YEAR LATER

I feel a tickle on my chest, and my eyes flutter open before my body jerks awake.

"Hey, relax." Hudson speaks in a hushed tone.

It takes a second for my eyes to adjust to our dim bedroom, and then panic sets in when I look down to see my daughter in my arms.

"It's okay, you fell asleep," my husband assures me with his hand resting on my shoulder from where he's standing next to our bed.

Grogginess fogs my brain, but I register that during feeding the baby I must have dozed off. Meanwhile, Grace Ruth seems to be at peace in my arms, alas awake, with her little eyes wide open. We call her Gracie for short.

"What time is it?"

Hudson brushes his finger along my bare breast to Gracie's cheek. "It doesn't matter. You go to bed and get some sleep. I'll take this one and burp her."

I blink my eyes a few times. "Hudson, you have to travel later for the game. I am positive you need more sleep than I do."

"Me going away is the very reason that you need a break now. Don't argue with me." His voice is soft yet firm as he coos at our daughter. "Mommy just needs to obey a little more."

A short laugh escapes me. "She may have you wrapped around her finger, but Mommy runs a tighter ship." I smile because Hudson and I have a tendency to speak in a saccharine tone around Gracie. It happened as soon as she was born, as if we were possessed.

Hudson begins to take our daughter out of my arms. "Go on. I'll see you at breakfast."

I yawn and reality hits me that I probably need an hour of shut-eye if I'll have any chance to survive the day. "Fine, Coach."

He is already patting her back as she rests her head against his shoulder, and he stares intently at Gracie. "Good girl, Piper."

Daddy Hudson is my undoing. He has an uncanny ability to sound so incredibly sexy, even when he is in full-on father-duty mode.

I begin to shuffle down and back under the covers of our bed. The moment that my head hits the pillow, I already feel sleep hitting me. Since Gracie is so young, and Hudson is in football season, I keep her in our room in one of those co-sleepers to avoid going back and forth, but we are evicting her as soon as she wakes less at night, and truthfully, she is growing so fast that she could use her crib too.

My eyes close, and I vaguely hear Hudson leave the room.

The next time I wake, I know the sun is up and it's morning. I have no idea how long I slept, but I take advantage of the fact that Hudson is downstairs with our daughter and decide to take a shower and throw on some makeup to accompany my yoga pants, t-shirt, and the mom-who-needs-sleep look. At least I know my bra is always sexy, even if I look a jumbled mess. I started a line of nursing bras, especially for my current state of life.

Heading down the stairs, I hear little noises from Gracie, and there's music on too. We have her on Bruce Springsteen in lullaby tones. I sigh when I see Hudson's suitcase by the front door as I walk to the kitchen. For the most part, we have found a routine, and we do our best to accommodate his schedule, but a lot of the away games are just too far for such a short period of time with the little one.

I smile at the view of Hudson leaning against the counter, drinking a smoothie, and making faces at our little girl in her bouncy chair. His eyes instantly turn to my direction when he notices me.

"Morning, beautiful."

I wave a hand in the air. "Get real with me. What time was it when you woke me earlier?"

He chuckles under his breath. "It was five, but just pretend it was eleven."

I groan as I grab a glass from the cupboard. If it was five, then it means I only got two more hours of sleep.

Hudson is quick to wrap his arms around me, take the glass from my hand, and pour me some smoothie. "Drew and Lucy said they could come up this weekend, even if I'm not here."

"When did they say that?"

"Check the family chat." He pulls his phone out of his

pocket and slides his thumb along the screen, then he shows me.

I smile brightly because Gracie is in her onesie that says Coach's Daughter and she seems at peace. He must have taken the photo earlier this morning, as it's the outfit she is wearing now, accompanied by Hudson's mug of coffee next to her that is one of those "world's greatest dad" mugs.

Drew wrote a message back.

DREW

> She's growing so quickly. Lucy and I want to come to babysit. This weekend? We can watch the game on the big screen.

Our daughter is a spoiled little girl. By everyone—her dad, brother, my grandmother, April, and I know I will be stopping by the baby aisle in the grocery store later when we don't need anything at all.

"I guess… well…" I'm reluctant, then Hudson gives me the pointed look. "Yes! Please send reinforcements my way," I admit with such relief.

I love motherhood, our routine, and our days together. But damn, this lack of sleep is a whole new world of crazy, and I welcome any opportunity for extra help.

Hudson smiles with reassurance. "Thought so. What's the plan for today?" He hands me a glass of green smoothie that I hate, but I know all the vitamins are exactly what I need, especially while breastfeeding.

The corners of my mouth stretch, and my face must look elated with happiness as I answer, "The usual. Pack up the stroller, stop in town to check on my boutique, then grab some lunch because I'm always starving these days, then naps, do laundry, afternoon walk, and sleep… hopefully."

"I will be back in two days," he reminds me.

"We'll be watching in the living room, I promise."

Hudson's fingers crawl up my arm, and he has a look that is the devil's good work. "We have a Sunday-afternoon game down in Kansas City. I'll be back late, but maybe Drew and Lucy can stick around Sunday night so I can take you to breakfast on Monday? Just you and me."

"I'd like that."

He leans his head down, and I stand on my toes to kiss him. "I'll miss you," he murmurs.

"Me too. But next week is a home game. We'll be there, and we are making this work. I promise to send you videos later today."

"Good." His phone gets a notification that his driver is here. He kisses me again, this time with more force and longer for good measure.

"I love you."

"I love you too, Mrs. Arrows."

We both look at our daughter who coos. Hudson is quick to go to Gracie and kiss her chubby cheek. "Of course, we love you too. Remember our talk earlier."

"Talk?" I wonder.

"The usual reminder that she is never to date athletes." He smiles at our daughter. "I'll be back soon. Be good for your mommy and protect her from pinecones."

"It was one time!" I protest.

"Yeah, and it knocked sense into you," he teases before ruffling our daughter's hair.

I wave a hand at him to get out of here, and exhale loudly, because even chaotic, life feels perfect lately.

———

AFTER HEADING TO TOWN, checking on my boutique where my staff was packing a bunch of orders, I went to the general store to pick up a salad at the deli counter and chatted with the old ladies from the knitting club who reminded me that there is a Lake Spark festival coming up. By the time I got home, I was ready for a long walk, so I put Gracie in a baby carrier and did my usual round up to the viewpoint and back.

But to my surprise, as I approach the house, I notice that April is parked on Spencer's driveway next door, and she is opening the trunk of her car.

"April?"

She looks at me as she swings a suitcase out of the back and her new beagle dog jumps out too.

"Oh, hey."

"Uhm. Think you parked at the wrong house. I wasn't expecting you. I mean, it's great, I just need to change the sheets in the guest room." I look down at my daughter, fast asleep.

April brings her hand to her hip and looks at me awkwardly. "I'm not here to stay with you."

"Right… then what are you here for?" Now I'm just confused.

April smiles tightly then bites her lip. "I'm… going to *temporarily* live with Spencer." Her hand comes to cover her face, as if she doesn't want to see me and would rather hide.

Which makes sense because I'm puzzled and don't understand. "As in my neighbor? The guy you hate? Wait, the guy who you actually call the asshole baseball player?"

"Yep." She pops the P with her lips.

"Why?" I ask blankly.

She nervously laughs. "Fun story. Or not. Remember your baby shower?"

"Of course." I smile because it was amazing. It was more

a party for Hudson and me. We did a gender reveal, had lunch at the Dizzy Duck Inn, ate cake, and Drew even made Hudson play ridiculous little games. It was a bigger event than our own wedding, which was a handful of people on the dock at the back of the house, a few weeks after Hudson proposed. "But what about the baby shower?"

She motions with her fingers to indicate size. "I might have made a teensy-weensy mistake with Spencer, and the man forgot to use the delete button. So, I need to hide out here in case the press figures it out." She speaks at the speed of light, but I heard a few keywords there.

When my jaw that went slack returns to normal position, I speak. "Oh my God!" I'm shocked but totally in a good way, well, minus the leaked-video part.

Her dog Pickles makes a whimpering sound, as if he agrees with me.

April waves at me. "Howdy, neighbor." She smiles weakly.

"We are *not* telling Hudson the specifics of this," I state.

"Please don't," she agrees.

I shake my head, but as I register everything, then a smile grows because I could kind of... see her and Spencer together.

"Oh, hey there, roomie," I hear Spencer call out as he appears to walk slowly with a swagger down his driveway.

April's face turns stiff, and she holds up her middle finger to him, but her eyes stay fixed on me. Her nostrils flare before smiling sweetly at me. "You'll be my alibi if a hot baseball player turns up at the bottom of Lake Spark?"

My grin doesn't fade. "I shouldn't highlight the fact that you just called him hot, should I?"

She grumbles as she starts her march in the direction of

her new temporary home, but I have a feeling it might not be temporary at all.

My phone vibrates in the pocket of the carrier, and I'm quick to pull it out to see a message from Hudson that he landed and already misses us. Glancing between my phone and a disgruntled April walking away, I chortle a laugh. They're the reminder that the best risks may just turn into something well worth it.

THANK YOU

Thank you for reading. It's you dear reader who makes this possible!

To Autumn, my life line for all my questions. Lindsay, who I've lost count how many books we've worked on together. Design Lindsey, I'm always in love with your creations.

Any blogger, advanced reader, and sharer who are all amazing and my gratitude can't be measured.

To my patient family, yeah, this writing thing? It's still happening!

Made in the USA
Coppell, TX
14 September 2024

37278654R00144